SLEAZELAND

ERASERHEAD PRESS
P.O. BOX 10065
PORTLAND, OR 97296

www.eraserheadpress.com
facebook/eraserheadpress

ISBN: 978-1-62105-275-3
Copyright © 2018 by Cody Goodfellow
Cover art copyright © 2018 Matthew Revert

Printed in the USA.

SLEAZELAND

CODY GOODFELLOW

ERASERHEAD PRESS
PORTLAND, OREGON

ZERO

[Cue: Felony, "The Fanatic"]

YOU GET OFF THE BUS—

The streets only look straight. You can't go two blocks without getting lost in a dream, into the settings of a thousand immortal scenes. Can't breathe without getting addicted. Every day here is equal to half a pack of cigarettes, they promise you. Work any job handling cash and you'll soak up enough crank, coke and molly to pop a piss test. If you're sad, just drink the tap water—it's got traces of Prozac and Zoloft in it.

The streets are named for everyone you ever loved or admired. This city is a movie and it's about you, but the street signs tell everyone their own story, so nobody can ever find each other, and no one can find the exit.

The world's dreams are made here, the most prized skins, lovingly tanned and hollowed out to make the hand puppets you thought were stars.

They show up at every audition. For every role, a hundred better versions of you. Waiting for every latte, a dozen manicured hands quicker, more qualified, tipping bigger than you. They all want something for nothing, and they'll do anything to get it.

Someday, if you give up everything but your dreams, if you never say die, but always kill, you'll become one of them.

And you know, one way or another, you'll never leave.

Your deflated body may hitch a ride or jump a bus back to nowhere, but the best part of you will always be here, haunting the endless gray snowy spaces between the commercials.

And even if your name never ends up in lights or on a street-sign or a star on Hollywood Boulevard, you know this town will never forget you, never stop loving you... until the next bus rolls in.

ONE

[Cue: Electric Light Orchestra, "Rockaria"]

YOU MAY NOT BE ABLE TO READ (no judgment here, reading is for losers), but I have no doubt you could give whoever's reading this to you an encyclopedia's worth of insights on how *not* to introduce the hero of a story.

Because you learned everything you know about real life from movies and TV, you may not realize that the earth orbits the sun or that your friend is fucking your significant other in real life, but you know the difference between net and gross points and have a keenly honed sense for the rigid cinematic code that visually establishes a protagonist's essential character to make them not merely plausible, but instantly sympathetic.

Someone to root for.

Encapsulate their outlook with a poignantly illustrative cameo of daily circumstance. Show, don't tell. When they wake up in the faded white farmhouse in the middle of the endless cornfield that stands for the lost American heartland, or under a crazy-wall flow-chart that grittily telegraphs all their tortured motivations.

When my theme music fires up, you'll see none of those shopworn cliches as I wake and crawl out of a bush in the precredit montage. You will squirm, starved for subliminal cues, and if you had any clout with the studio, you'd probably try to talk me out of showing you how this morning, I beat a man nearly to death with his own dog.

My name is Charlie Parsons, a.k.a. Chaz Parrish (commercial and promotional work), Chuy Pastrana (*telenovela*, nonunion background and stunt) and Chuck Parker (gay porn). I'm not like everyone else in this town. I need to be believed more than I need to be liked.

Cue opening theme music—classic, aspirational to the point of irony. The foot-stomping heritage rock anthem drives a quick-cut intro to our down & out but irrepressible urchin, styling and jiving half a step ahead of the jaws of the indifferent world looking to chew off his ass…

My head pops out of a bush on the perimeter of MacArthur Park by the Levitt Pavilion bandshell, as seen in *Killer Bait*, *The Hidden*, *Falling Down*, *Kiss Kiss Bang Bang* and *Volcano*. It's a shitty place to sleep, but there's always a location shoot at Park West, the defunct hotel across the street, and the PA's never try to guess if the street-trash pawing the craft service tables are real homeless or non-union extras "playing homeless."

I dart across the street between Star Wagons—a bad sign, if this wasn't a shit gig, they'd have the newer Quixote trailers—and sneak into the background dressing room for a quick moist towelette bath, and change into the least pungent set of street clothes the actors left behind. I emerge to pinch my morning coffee, a cinnamon roll, blueberry Yoplait yogurt, a bunch of green grapes and half a flagon of rancid Dole pineapple juice. Slim pickings, not even an omelet bar, but the important part of passing for background is to look totally indifferent.

Background is a sweet gig if you can't pull anything weightier, but it's no place for real actors. They're the ones always angling for more face time, for a line and a SAG letter, the ones who make life hell with their bitching about the poor treatment and lousy food, compared to the principals and the crew, and even the for-fuck's-sake stand-ins.

Background gets the careful, if not caring, treatment of supplementary evidence in a criminal trial, and it chafes on them because they want to be pampered. These miserable

CODY GOODFELLOW

people want to be actors, not necessarily to act, and will never be satisfied. They should be killed quietly and left to rot whenever you can get away with it.

The competition even to be human furniture in this town is ferocious. But if you just want to act, there are always unorthodox opportunities for the young thespian still perfecting his craft. Watching the game trail from my favorite blind in a hibiscus bush, I consume my scavenged bounty and watch for my designated prey.

Looks like a hep Kennedy-era Freedom Rider in his vintage bottle-green sharkskin suit and tortoise-shell hornrims, but his earlobes still droop like shot rubber bands halfway to his collar from his last hipster incarnation. He's thumbing the news and making a big show of not noticing his dog grunting out a missile the size of the Chrysler Building.

This dog owner neither likes nor believes me when I drop out of the tree and fall in behind him, asking him politely in my best indoor voice to clean up after his dog.

Nobody you will ever meet in LA has empathy or a decent backyard. They're all cat people, but they need a worshipful fan, so they all have dogs. He looks elaborately offended without acknowledging me at all, as if reading about the poop incident in his news feed. He kneels to bag the half-kilo of feces in a green plastic carbon-neutral bag, ties it neatly, and puts it back on the sidewalk, archived for posterity not ten feet from where I was sleeping.

I didn't ask to be real homeless. Some might see it as a symptom of general failure in my profession, but homelessness is an essential element of preparation for the actor's life. Homeless people typically go for weeks at a time without being addressed by name or otherwise treated like a human being, which is psychologically devastating for the layman, but vital seasoning for the would-be actor.

Anyone who tells you confidence is important is selling you down the river. Confidence comes away from the audition sure they'll call because you *nailed* it, while craven, howling insecurity scarfs an eight-ball and lurks in the bushes in a

Catwoman outfit, which, Sean Young aside, has worked a lot more times than it has failed.

It's almost as hard to be homeless, as it is to be a working actor. Time was, this city was dotted with all-night theaters where you could sleep, tweak or jack off to professional-quality pornography with some modicum of dignity like the churches used to let you do, when they still cared.

But I digress.

I ask him who is supposed to pick up the (admittedly, attractively packaged) shit, if not the dog's owner?

He tells me to fuck off and starts walking away.

I ask him to pick it up before I do.

He walks faster.

I pick up the shit and go jogging after him. It's not even 8 and it's already ninety-two, and everyone on the street who can't afford a personal climate system is swimming in their own gravy.

I catch up with him half a block later.

I ask him to open his mouth.

He tells me to fuck off again and his breath is redolent of onions, fennel toothpaste and unaddressed gum disease. In spite of all this, I tell him again to open his mouth and he kicks the dog and says, *Kill.*

Seriously, to the dog: *Kill!*

The dog's way out of this guy's weight class, a Rottweiler mix and somewhere, at least one breeder got down and threw some human genes into the batter and they took, because the dog's got fucking *hips.* It has *shoulders.*

If the dog was smarter, he'd be on my side. But generations of breeding and judicious beatings win out and the dog lunges at me.

Now it should—nay, it must—be said that I love dogs, probably more than you. My second longest foster father said that any man with a good dog didn't need a gun to kill at will, but his wife wouldn't let him own a gun or hit the dog, and the dog ended up eating his face when he had a stroke and couldn't feed it.

I feint left, then jump right, take the leash from the asshole and swing the dog by its fancy three-point harness over my head and I bring it down hard on the guy's shoulders two or three more times before he goes down and the dog runs away and the asshole *still* doesn't want to open his mouth, not even to say *I'm sorry*.

I notice then that one of his eyes is filling up with blood from the inside. I ask him if he needs anything. He pats himself down for his phone, or maybe he's just twitching.

I ask if there's anything else I can do. He asks me to take care of his dog. I tell him that ship has sailed, to make peace with the universe closing the book on his life as a vivid if unsubtle reminder to others to clean up after their pets in public. He tells me to fuck off again, and his eyes go blank without apologizing and YOU TELL ME WHO WON BECAUSE I DON'T KNOW.

If this proves anything about me, I'd hope it goes to show my willingness to sacrifice the literal for the ideal. I am but an instrument of my audience and fate. Presented with the bare minimum society demanded of him, he chose anarchy, and reaped a whirlwind.

Guilt is like that reflex when you wake up with a sore throat, and you swallow constantly to see if it's *really* a viral invasion, or just rawness from heat and pollution and blowjobs, or just excessive nervous swallowing, and you swallow and you swallow to determine if it's going away, or if it's the first twinkling of esophageal polyps or thyroid tumors, and your swallowing induces cobblestone calluses down the throat to the lungs and you die from undiagnosed cancer of the salivary gland.

Running for the bus, I know they're going to get me; and when they finally run me down, and these four frustrated pro wrestlers stage an impromptu *auto da fe* across the hood of the Mercedes convertible with two parking tickets jammed under the windshield wipers, not one motorist will shed a tear for the failure of civilization being staged for their entertainment.

So as I pass, I grab the tickets off the Mercedes and as I run westbound on Wilshire, I stuff them in my mouth, tear off a big shred and choke it down.

It's hard to run barefoot faster than four highly motivated

policemen, and even more so while dry-swallowing the forty-pound, semi-waterproof traffic citations issued by the LA County Parking Enforcement junta.

But I remember what my voice-acting mentor told me in workshop, about attaching personal mental pictures to the script in your head. If you can visualize the right pictures during an audition, you can totally command the tone, so a D.A.R.E. PSA about crystal meth makes kids hungry for drugs, or a sunny California Lottery ad carries the subtle aftertaste of impending ruination and doom that sends rubes scrambling for scratch-n-wins.

Commit to your pictures and SELL them. It doesn't matter what the script says, it doesn't matter whether you know the words to the song or not, if you can fake the feeling.

Confident, handsome upscale actor/casualwear catalog model on his way to a promising audition. See him strolling down the street with a script in one hand and soy chai latte in the other. Slim white jeans, distressed vintage Steely Dan tour shirt and raw silk keffiyeh elaborately knotted round his neck. Hair still spiky-wet from a shower and a discreet palmful of product with the merest hint of vanilla scent, a smile for everyone I pass that leaves them floating in their shoes and taking out their phones, itchy to buy something.

The trick is not to con the mark. Sell yourself to yourself, and all the world lines up to buy.

These are the kinds of lessons you only learn at the workshops when you run out of money, but refuse to leave. These are invaluable lessons that only cost me everything.

I stop running. I don't look behind me, though I can hear them getting closer. I turn and ask the cops if they know the bus lines at all and they stop running and they look at me strange and then at each other.

I walk away and I wonder what they see when they look at me, because when I look at them now, they're not even cops. Just more actors in costumes, late for an audition.

I board the bus and sit down next to a sleeping housekeeper,

CODY GOODFELLOW

moving her big Nordstrom shopping bag of cleaning supplies onto the floor and taking her phone out of her purse. I have a lot of bad luck with phones, but everybody else has one, and they'll share if you ask nice.

My agent says she's got nothing for me, but to try back in an hour. I give the housekeeper back her phone and pull the cord for the next stop as we cross Melrose.

In spite of all the ugliness and turbulence of the morning, I am buoyed up by the unshakable sense that someone, somewhere, is going to hire me.

TWO

[Cue: Lemon Jelly, "Homage to Patagonia"]

IT'S HARD TO STAY POSITIVE IN THIS TOWN. The desperation of making it is so suffocating that the first incidental mote of validation will leave you tripping so hard you don't notice you're still starving, like some delirious desert-island castaway so grateful for solid food, you don't realize you're greedily eating your own bony ass with both hands.

If you've never been here, I'll save you the trouble. Remember that Sara McLachlan song in *Toy Story 2*, about a world of toys made to crave love, yet doomed to abandonment and self-loathing by the fickle vicissitudes of cruel childhood? Now picture a landfill with five million broken, defective toys and burnt-out lightbulbs, used condoms and broken toilet brushes that somehow convinced themselves that they were also wonderful toys, limping around lamenting how they never got played with in rambling Broadway numbers, in between unfulfillingly fucking each other and rehearsing Mamet monologues.

To weather all this negativity, you need more than a dream. You've got to have someone in your corner, someone who knows the ropes, and you've got to have a plan.

Forget Stanislavski, Strasberg, Adler and Hagen. Fuck Brando, Dean, Franco, Cruise and all your idols. However unpromising my present circumstances may look, I don't even want to imagine where I'd be without *Spoiled Rotten: The Short Life And Bizarre Enigma Of A Little Hollywood Monster*, and not just because it's the only book without pictures that I've ever read.

Remember that asshole child star from that one commercial and that lame basic cable sitcom, who got so pissed at his outtakes airing on blooper shows, that he started swearing like a hog auctioneer with Tourette's whenever he didn't like the way a take was going? The one who allegedly drugged and sexually assaulted his TV mom, so the show got cancelled and never picked up for syndication? The one who sued his parents, then tried to hire a hit man to kill them when they cut up his credit cards, then tried to commit suicide, but his parents replaced his pills with candy? The one who accused his agent, the producers and costars of his TV series of molesting him, but finally fessed up that he made up the whole thing to blackmail them into giving him work?

Remember his name? Shiva? Sativa? Shinobi! Yeah, Shinobi Honeycutt. What a douchebag, right?

I forgive you if you don't remember the name, or only remember him as a mildly amusing cautionary tale; but that, my friend, is why you always lose. If more wanna-be's were familiar with the criminally underrated acting gifts and ingenious image management of the most notorious child star of the mid-nineties, then the competitive intensity around here would make Hollywood as it is today look like a utopian ashram.

My only physical possession when I first came to Hollywood was a dog-eared copy of *Spoiled Rotten* a good-natured trucker gave me in return for a lackluster handjob at a rest stop in Oklahoma, and it sealed my destiny. I carried it with me everywhere, read it until the binding disintegrated, and then carried loose, heavily highlighted pages in my wallet, dispensing particularly pithy slices of wisdom to waiters and less enlightened colleagues in lieu of cash tips. People I thought I could save.

Say what you will about his problematic resume and personality, but if you want to be nothing more than a puppet who wastes away dreaming of having a series of strangers' hands up your ass, you go right ahead and base your life on the teachings of anyone but Shinobi Honeycutt. See where it gets you.

Any pretender can put himself into someone else's shoes. More of a *reality artist*, a true actor puts the whole world into HIS shoes.

From *Spoiled Rotten*, page 173:

> Precocious far beyond his years, eight-year old Shinobi reacted against the stressful, highly controlled environment of *The Persons* set and explored his curiosity about the human body in ways that soon got tiresome for his costars. "One thing I learned real fast," said Maureen Heasley, the third actress to play "Vanessa," the teenaged older sister on the troubled show, "was don't bend over within arm's reach of that little shit."
>
> No one was safe from Shinobi's fascination with bottoms, which some attribute to the ill-advised gift of a copy of *Everybody Poops* by his on-set educator; recordings of Shinobi tirelessly quoting the book at inappropriate moments, at least, should put paid to enduring rumors he never learned to read.
>
> Male and female costars alike, as well as crew and even unwary reporters and network execs were equally at risk of finding a child's index finger inserted where they appreciated it least while they were trying to do their jobs. Many costars who declined to be interviewed candidly admitted that they ignored the uninvited probing as much as they could in the interest of keeping the budget-troubled show on schedule.
>
> But this enduring rumor paints a very different picture of the impudent young actor from the infamous and almost certainly apocryphal story that Honeycutt, suddenly a worldly prepubescent Lothario on his ninth birthday, successfully seduced his TV mother, Shirley Berthel, at an Ace Awards banquet, and that she subsequently aborted his child, precipitating her nervous breakdown and withdrawal from the show…

In an age when most kids were accidents, the damage from proteins traded like paint between sleepy commuters on the turnpike, Shinobi Honeycutt was named before he was conceived, shaped for a singular destiny, groomed to be his household's sole provider before he could walk. Conditioned to burn out before puberty.

But in every way available to him, Shinobi cut his own strings and danced to his own tune, and when the time came for him to become a human sacrifice, he vanished on his own terms, leaving the stage an enigma, and thus immortal wherever 30-something losers held hostage to nostalgic dreck trade bootleg DVD's. It's easy to stand in judgment on an eight-year old kid who blew a career anyone else would kill for by sticking his fingers in people's butts, but step into the arena, and you'll realize why we do what we do, and you'll see that every awful thing Shinobi Honeycutt did, he did for you.

As for the plan part…

While I've yet to close the deal on a speaking part in any film or video production since coming to Hollywood __ years ago, I've been attached to several hundred projects of varying quality and artistic merit, and had a hand in developing many of the most successful motion pictures, television programs and engineered celebrity scandals in recent years.

Uncredited, naturally. And everyone knows about Hollywood math. When it comes time to pay up, no major motion picture has ever claimed a final net profit for tax purposes.

Like everybody, I was really naïve about how things get done when I first came out here, and desperately stupid, even when I did know better. I used a lot of crank to make it through hustling, and every minute I didn't have something in my mouth, I ran pitches out of it, thinking one of these guys would suddenly look at me the way the farmer looked at Orville when Charlotte spelled out SOME PIG in cobwebs over his pen, and instead of a breath mint and an In N Out gift certificate by way of a tip, I'd be whisked off to Richard Lim to be measured for a new wardrobe, and then to a studio. It didn't work out that way, but I know some of those fuckers stole my work.

When I was young and still had stars in my eyes, I printed this up and left it out for producers to read in the stalls at the Viper Room. Degrading and repellent, sure, but it was a simpler time, and it beat trying to get their attention in an elevator. It has shown up twice on the Blacklist under other titles. Several A-listers have been attached, but it's one of those dangerously important ideas everybody wants to see somebody else make. I'm still looking for someone to help me flesh out the treatment, but everything you'd need to seal the deal is right here.

Feisty smalltown trans teen runaway comes to the big city and hustles in drag to collect enough money to pay for the operation, and then seize her dream of becoming a champion lady ultimate fighter and battle the reigning champion, only to discover that her opponent is the mom who abandoned her when she was a teenager, herself.

Think about it: the two ultimate human ideals combined in one gripping, tragic human story. The journey from whore to boxer is the ultimate modern human struggle, and surefire Oscar-bait. And if the operation actually goes down during shooting, the lead can be nominated for Best Actor *and* Best Actress, and they haven't made an ego in Hollywood that can resist a cheap political point like that. Only an inhuman monster like Mel Gibson would vote against it.

Just say the word and show me the money, and I'll start getting the shots…

THREE

[CUES: Yma Sumac, "The Sun Virgins"; Robert Palmer, "Johnny & Mary"]

EVERY YEAR, TEN THOUSAND PEOPLE DISAPPEAR in America, or maybe a hundred thousand just in the greater SoCal region… depends on how shitty and careless is the horror movie or true crime tabloid show that drops the statistic. They're not in a roadside ditch or in a reservoir or at the center of a crazy elaborate crime scene concocted by a diabolical genius to drive a cop on the edge into madness and gnarly Old Testament revenge.

Look for them on your fucking TV. They're right here. You can see them all day long if you stay home and look past the cockeyed daytime talkshow host and scan the audience.

The topics for the shows they're shooting this morning are posted on the wall behind the lady with the clipboard. She asks me if I have any preconceived notions or strong opinions about feminine Viagra. I don't answer right away. I just tear up.

Visualize the pictures.

Feel the feelings.

Burn the pictures.

Picture the fully-stocked brunch buffet in the commissary, with an omelet station and waffle bar.

But not for you…

Picture ketchup packets and dumpster hash browns behind

Highland McDonalds.

"My wife was a test case," I tell her. "I don't know if I can say anything, it's so raw, and it still might end up in court…" She's salivating so hard, I'm worried I gave her spit-cancer.

"At first, it was wonderful. She was able to do it, actually *wanted* to, but then… the side effects kicked in…"

I start crying again. The line behind me is complaining. She takes me aside and has an intern screen the rubes.

What side effects, please? Take your time… Would you like a mocha, or some bottled water? She holds up a Pellegrino. The rest of the cattle are drinking generic Kirkland so hot, the plastic bottles have started to dissolve into the water. Drink enough of it, and you won't ever need to inject caulk into your dumper.

She's tipped her hand. I angle for a cash spiff. "Turned me out of the house… I can't even afford to hire a lawyer, and I'm ashamed to go to the police…"

She forces the clipboard on me to write it down. A twenty so clean and new it feels like a linen dinner napkin tickles my sweaty palm.

"Her… her *thing*," I say… "The… joy buzzer, the man in the boat?" Her *clitoris*?

I start bawling again. I can't write it down, I can barely say it, barely nod and then breathlessly whisper, "*It grew.*"

The intern's bawling, too, the cattle are stampeding to get at the sucker-bait buffet. I console myself with thrice-reheated buffalo wings, sucking the blubber and gristle off seven stunted bone skewers slathered in generic ranch dressing before I compose myself to go on.

Long story short, her clit grew into an eight-inch cock. Longer than mine but slimmer, like a dog's dick. And when she got excited, which was often, it swelled up and turned a livid, priapic purple, and she forced herself on me again and again, and I'd have to rub ice on it to get it to retract back into its sheath…

Have you ever told anyone else about this? If you'd be willing…
"Oh, I never could…"
But if you could share your story, they'd help you, you might

CODY GOODFELLOW

even be able to get pro bono legal representation…

"I don't blame her, you understand, I know she was just responding to something beyond her control. She was like an animal with her eyes rolled back in her head, and that unnatural monster dog-dick using her, abusing me and making a mockery of the natural order and of our love. If these modern women want equality, well, there it is, they'll finally have everything they think they want…"

I can tell from her eyes I'm laying it on too thick, so I devolve back into tearful brooding as she checks her phone. *Is she with you here today?*

I look back down the line and shake my head tersely, as if shushing someone, then I look back guiltily, eyes downcast to my left, emoting dishonesty. *No, she's not here.*

She says stay put, goes to find the line producer.

I've worked 1,283 studio audiences in my career. Right now, my pitch is sending panty splashes up and down the production chain of command, but I know how it's going to end. They'll interview me in a phony green room after plying me with boxed wine and rubbery shrimp cocktail, surreptitiously record and transcribe it and give my life story to a temp from Central Casting, someone more telegenic, someone less (as the more edifying comment cards I've gleaned off a lifetime shoulder-surfing PA's clipboards) "sweaty," "clanky," or "desperate."

If they're feeling generous, I might get fifty bucks, sign a false name on a release, and fill my pockets on the way out with leftover shrimp. But when any encounter is a chance to be absorbed into the godhead of celebrity, you can never give up. Failure to try is just like firing yourself, cutting your own throat. At least make them do it for you.

So I know I won't be missing much when I wander out of line to see the commotion in the next corral.

This barely legal girl is talking animatedly, conjuring lightning with her hands, telling the nonplussed junior assistant producer of an even lower-rent talk show than the one I'm auditioning for something that makes some of the people around her stare in awe, while others clear their throats for something solid to spit on her.

She's pretty in that sturdy, Kate Winslet way that so few American actresses can pull off, imbued with that lusty peasant quality that flourishes and withers out here like a wild rose on a radiator.

Her smile raises goosebumps on my arms. She can't be quite eighteen. She's also pregnant, riding high and narrow like it's sure to be a boy. A couple trimesters later than I usually like, her navel popped like the meat thermometer in a turkey.

I can't look away. It's not just that I have a sickness for the thickness or severe pheromone susceptibility, or that she's dyed her hair with that hot magenta, cherry-cola hue that'd inspire me to fuck a mop that's been dipped in it. To defuse the sexual tension, I picture her as a guy, but if she was a guy, she'd be a chubby Ryan Gosling, and I'd still pay to fuck his shoes.

The producers humor her for a few more minutes, until security comes over and escorts her out of the rope line.

I brace one of the tryouts lurking in her wake. "Another virgin birth," he says. "Like, seriously? Go back to '99."

Yes, please let's do…

If I was smooth, I'd come at her with the twenty and go, *Hey girl, did you drop this?* But I just follow her, lurking and relishing every chance to step on her shadow. She's almost off the lot, the security checkpoint and the sidewalk, when I go, "If you're working the paternity test angle, you need at least two baby-daddies to get them to put you on."

She looks back over her shoulder and smiles at *me*.

My goosebumps all lay eggs.

I know that smile. Relief when they see I'm not as scary as I sounded. No threat at all. "No big deal," she goes. "I was just trying to get tested for free."

"You know who the father is?"

"Oh, I *know*… I mean, it was definitely supernatural… But like, not a shower of gold, or a swan, you know, like in a Greek myth? But damn… How hot would that be, to be raped by a swan?"

My classical education is for shit, so I change the subject. "I could be a baby-daddy if you want to go on. They know me. I've done the whole circuit. We just need to get a *real* freak to be the heel… I know a bunch of those, if you got a phone."

"That's alright, thanks." No reproach, no hope, no fear.

"So, you act much, before you came out here?"

"Oh, God no. Actors are fucking flakes."

"I know, right? I could tell you some stories—"

"I've got *real* skills. I'm a music supervisor."

I snort before I catch myself. She's dead serious. There are a lot of jobs in Hollywood that require technical certification, union or guild membership or superhuman people-reading, communication and manipulative skills. There are many entry-level dead-end jobs that demand only total dedication to wearing yourself down like a human eraser, rubbing away shreds of disposable soul with every thankless task. And then there are dead-easy, retarded, plum jobs that require no measurable skill whatsoever, and so are inevitably passed out as spoils of nepotism. Faceless nobodies with famous surnames abound, and the pinnacle of the field is that one totally useless asshole who got invited to every party at your school.

Pick an appropriate recorded song for a scene and tell legal to negotiate the clearance; congratulations, you've successfully supervised the music.

Every douche with an iTunes account thinks he can DJ, and music supervisory is DJing, without the reflexes or charisma. Among shiftless but well-connected shitheels, music supervisor is the *sine qua non* of all bitchin' jobs. Club DJs, coke dealers, ex-radio jocks, yoga instructors, gigolos, nephews, nieces, cousins, shiftless, barely-legal boy-toys with permanently dislocated jaws.

"So… what song would you play under *this* scene?" I try to float it like a bad check, scribbled in crayon. "All the noise and nonsense and crazy, desperate people…"

She smiles. My goosebumps take flight. "I don't know… I

suppose, if you weren't talking so much, something loose, naive and whimsically downbeat, like Kid Koala…"

"I don't know them," I almost blurt out, but bite my lip. Just nod sagely.

"OK, if that's too obscure for you… More driving cadence, but more eye-level… 'Crush' by Sleigh Bells… What would you use?"

Is she flirting with me? I look around. "OK, how about 'Jungle,' by ELO…"

"Maybe if this was a period piece. *Do you know anything from your own lifetime?*"

I smile. "How old do you think I am?"

She squints. "Kinda old, I guess… but… Seriously? That's like, my grandmother's music."

"Shame on you. Electric Light Orchestra is the apotheosis of everything pure and true about classical, pop rock and disco, fused in catchy, cinematically vivid tunes."

"Wow," she says. What choice does she have?

"I change my pick. 'Rockaria,' yeah. It's about this cocky dude who thinks he's going to shake up this really square chick's world, because she's into classical music…"

Her smile widens, giving me a sliver of real hope. "And what happens next?"

"They go do lunch?"

She bats her lashes. Sad pout. "Thanks, no… I'm just gonna catch a ride to the clinic…"

"You *can't*." I get in front of her. I try to be taller. "I don't even think you can, as late as you are…"

She looks offended. "I didn't come all this way just to get scraped, dummy. White babies are worth teen coin in LA. I'm selling it on craigslist and getting a motorcycle."

"Are you fucking with me?"

She smiles like she doesn't already own me. Like my heart isn't hanging out of my chest, a flapping chicken with its neck in a noose.

And then I hear the Voice.

I AM THE ONE

I look around, unsure if I really heard it, or if it's the voices again. Everybody in the crowd checking their phone or chewing each other's ears off. A big-headed little black guy in a raincoat fishes water bottles out of the trash. I stick my fingers in my ears and dig out some waxy buildup and soap crust.

DELIVER ME FROM MY ENEMIES

This doesn't sound like *my* voices. My voices sound like Ken Nordine doing spoken word, or Ernie Anderson, the guy who did all the ABC bumpers through the 70's and 80's. They narrate what I'm doing when I get confused, as if it's a Movie of the Week promo.

I CAME BACK TO EARTH TO BRING HARMONY TO ALL HUMANKIND

I say, "I want to help you."

Who writes this shit? Says Ernie.

This shit writes us, answers Ken.

Looking at her phone. "What can you do for me?"

"I… I've been around. I know things… people… I can help you…"

Give it up, loser, barks Ernie.

Give it in, winner, purrs Ken.

"With what?"

"Did you mean… what you said back there… about it being a virgin…?"

"Did you mean what you said back there about your girlfriend's clitoris?"

"NO… That? How'd you even…?"

A big black SUV pulls up to the curb, the windows triple-tinted so the occupants look like cave fish in an aquarium filled with espresso. Three big bald, swarthy guys stuffed into a single charcoal gray worsted wool suit climb out, yelling at the driver and uttering, in the whole exchange, not a single fucking vowel.

She's leaving, and I have nothing to lose. I can't resist. I reach out and put my hand on her belly.

The voice shoots up my arm like pissing on a fifty thousand

watt radio transmitter.

MEN WILL RISE AGAINST YOU DEMONS WILL TRY TO DEVOUR YOU BUT IF YOU BELIEVE IN ME YOU WILL BE TRANSFORMED THE WORLD WILL EVOLVE AND HEAVEN AND EARTH WILL BE ONE

The girl accepts a massive paw that assists her into the back seat and the three guys in the single suit punch me in the gut so hard they've run the light and jumped onto 101 North before my ass hits the pavement.

I fall down a nameless Hollywood hustler, believer in nothing, but I arise a righteous disciple, harbinger of a new golden age. That teenage runaway's unborn bastard baby is the One True God, and I am its chosen prophet.

So this is love.

FOUR

[Cue: Giorgio Moroder, "Paul's Theme (Jogging Chase)"]

PEOPLE ALWAYS ASK ME HOW I CAME BY MY doggedly positive outlook. How could you stay the course and keep feeding the dream after over twenty years, 3,200 audition rejections, and being attached to exactly 957 scrapped, failed, unfinanced or shelved projects, and getting shitcanned off 194 more?

Unless I'm trying to get laid, I never tell them the truth.

I let them suppose I just had the right kind of upbringing to engender such unshakable confidence, or that I've known the depths of despair, but vowed never to let any petty obstacle break my stride, or occasionally that I'm just severely brain-damaged. Depends on my mood. But I'm protecting them.

Good, decent American folks, people who want to go to church and feel good about it, should go their whole lives without learning about Operation Bethlehem.

Nobody knows, but best guess is that they started right after *Roe v. Wade*, and carried on until they either disbanded or quietly imploded without forcing the government to admit that they ever existed, about ten years ago.

When a female who fit the profile went in for an abortion in the kind of state where people line up outside the last surviving clinic to harangue and berate them up to the door, she came out of the mandatory orientation meeting where she met the vacuum cleaner, had an invasive ultrasound and was forced to write a name on a pink or blue near-birth announcement to be mailed to her parents before she could schedule an appointment for the actual scraping (your state may not have such laws, and you may or may not agree with their politics, but without them, the person reading this to you might not be here today); but then she was shoved out the side entrance with a bag over her head by a Bethlehem-friendly nurse, and was thrown into a van.

She wakes in a basement in a strange house in a nowhere town upstate. If she cooperates, the next few months pass smoothly. She is induced as soon as the fetus is viable, then allowed to recover while some hypnosis and light psychic driving is used to make her forget where she's been or what really happened.

She got scraped and went on a binge, and if she just shuts up and pockets the money, everybody gets on with their lives, the grand design unfolds, and God is served. I never heard of any mothers acting up, but if they did, who'd listen? Only us.

Some of us are adopted through liaisons with churches who screen their parents and help them covertly adopt the babies as their own, even down to providing cover stories for the unexpected arrival and falsified blood tests. But some of us are raised as brothers in a network of underground orphanages that make ancient Sparta look like Sandals. We learn the Bible. Psalm 127.4. We are arrows in the hand of a mighty man. We learn to kill with our bare hands and live on thistle and recycled sweat. We learn gratitude.

Though I was groomed to take up the cause, to roam the red states, the flyover wastelands, looking for bowlegged teen mothers to abduct to fill the gaping quivers of God's chosen, now I am called to infiltrate this godforsaken industry on a quest to find a reality TV producer with the vision to bring the story of my people to basic cable and all premium streaming platforms.

So yeah, my motivations are pretty one-dimensional, and I'm comfortable with that.

CODY GOODFELLOW

FIVE

[CUES: Speedy West, "West Of Samoa"; Pet Shop Boys, "Suburbia"; *The Persons*—Opening Theme]

MY AGENT LIVES WITH THREE DOGS AND A turtle in a Saracen fifth wheel parked under the 101 overpass on Vine, just up the street from the iconic Capitol Records tower and the Palace, where Groucho Marx hosted *You Bet Your Life* from 1950 to 1960. Fifteen percent of my net doesn't pay for coffee, but Mimi Murishige believes in me, and she has other revenue streams. She has the only trained Valhalla's Celtic Lurcks in LA.

Hideous, hairless things like Great Dane skeletons dipped in candle wax, with outgrown dewclaws that, if not docked at birth, tend to go full opposable. And unlike most purebred dogs, they only get more fiendishly clever and dexterous with inbreeding. So much so that the few reckless weirdoes who actually breed them tend to have the studs' eyes put out. The Valhalla's Celtic Lurck breeder subculture would make for a great opera.

When I climb into the passenger seat, one of them is gobbling down a bowl of raw eggs, yogurt and oysters, while the other one smokes a menthol cigarette in a special holder Mimi made for them.

"You got anything to eat?"

"If you can get it away from Xerxes, go for it." She takes a monster hit off a gigantic UC Santa Cruz bong shaped like a banana slug.

Mimi works with entertainers at all levels, and showers upon us nurturing love and wisdom irrespective of our earning potential. When I first came to town, I tried to bang everything that moved. She told me this trick to free myself of sexual tension, because lust is only a distraction when you're broke and powerless, and nobody you want will touch you for free.

When you're turned on by a very special lady, just focus on her eyes and the nose, and only there. Everyone who is born female could've gone the other way if not for the whims of hormones or the acidity of the uterine environment or some shit, and vice versa. Focus on the features, and it's easy to picture any woman as a man, and vice versa. So easy to see them with the opposite plumbing and chemistry, and then remember how little banging strangers matters in the larger arena of life, and you can focus on what they're saying instead of losing yourself in fantasies. As a sexual omnivore, it never really sets me completely free from desire. (If she was a man, Mimi would be Sammo Hung, and even she's not always safe.) But judicious reworking of her tactic makes it easier when, in the course of my work, I have to blow really gross guys. When flipping their sex doesn't help, I just picture them as injured animals in a really sick petting zoo.

"I've got some webseries work, but you won't make the cut, trust me." She coughs up silver frozen smoke. "Every scene with more than four extras this season is a nightclub or a prison yard, and you don't fit either."

"So why am I here?"

"Nobody knows, darling. How was the park gig?"

"It was good…"

"Good?"

"I did what you said to do. *I* was stellar. The guy I worked with… not so much. Is he really dead?"

"Even better, he's in a coma. You made the morning local news. AM radio is shitting their pants about purging the homeless

CODY GOODFELLOW

population, but Piolin is already doing a Yanqui Piñata contest. You have to bust open a white papier-mâché Yuppie with a dog from a local shelter to win tickets to see Pitbull."

"*I* should be on there."

"You should be in Tijuana until this blows over. Have you seen your composite sketch?"

She shows me on her phone. We have a good laugh, then she says, "Yeah… you're probably going to have to change your name again."

"How the fuck am I supposed to build a resume, if I have to keep changing my identity?"

She shrugs. It's barely ten percent of a shrug.

"Now will you get me a real audition?"

I get the other ninety percent of the shrug.

"What about background work?"

She slashes me with an eyebrow. "You never *stay* in the background. But I've got some more pickup reality work…"

"God, no."

"A studio suit needs someone to fellate a recurring guest star on a tier-3 sitcom on-camera for salary negotiation collateral. Bonus if they get the target going downtown…"

"Pass…"

"You don't want to see the headshot first?"

"…Pass."

"The Hollywood Merchants' Association wants someone to dress up as Spider Man and assault the Viacom characters out in front of the Chinese."

"That always ends well… What else?"

"Phil from ADT is always looking for home invaders…"

"No."

"He's got a thing with the deputy sheriffs, now. You won't get picked up, and if you do…"

Phil's a home security salesman; he has guys break into the houses of prospects who turn him down on his door-to-door rounds. Bust into the house the next day and vandalize, desecrate, defecate, loot and pillage, threaten the housekeeper so she quits, and generally fulfill every homeowner's worst nightmare so they sift the wreckage looking for Phil's card. But Phil's last prospect lied about owning firearms.

And then I'm like, "So, hey… speaking of *security*… You know anything about a personal security company with, like a bloody red bird for a logo?"

"Dear God, no… Who'd you get in a fight with, now?"

"Nobody. His client was talking to me, and he just hit me, like out of fucking nowhere…"

"You're lucky not to be talking out of a tube."

"Always. But like… Are they bodyguards, or what?"

"They're motherfuckers. Blood Eagle Security. You know what a blood eagle is?"

"Merit badge you get in Eagle Scouts for barebacking a girl on the rag."

"Wrong," she says, somehow making three syllables out of it. "Fuck-pig. It's some barbaric Slavic thing, where they cut slots in the back of your ribcage and pull your lungs out so they dangle like wings.

"Worst of all," she concludes, "they're Transnistrian."

"What's that, another cult?"

"So much worse. It's a phony country. Breakaway Moldovan territory, a clearinghouse for smuggling and drugs and weapons and shit. They're like Serbs, but worse."

"What's wrong with Serbs?"

The dogs growl. The one behind the wheel flicks its cigarette butt at me. "Nothing," Mimi hedges, "as a people. You've seen their movie, right? Not all of them ran rape camps or collected the ears of Croat refugees. Not all of them wormed out of war crimes charges and moved over here to run prostitutes and Balkan snuff films, or opened a personal security company that represents people who should be killed by lightning, or a giant foot coming down from Heaven. I'm sure some of them are wonderful human beings."

"So… you know them pretty well?"

"What do you want with those evil pieces of shit?"

"There's a girl…"

Waggling her eyebrows and wrinkling her nose, finally intrigued, Mimi takes a big plutonium-colored sativa weed-tumor out of a blue snap-can like tennis balls come in, drops it in a coffee grinder, then packs the resulting evil purple dust into the bong. "You mean a literal little girl, or are you objectifying her?"

"I think she's in trouble."

"More trouble than *you*?"

"Yeah."

"Then forget her," she says, firing the bong and coughing up a moaning Victorian ghost. "OK," she finally says, "last chance. Kevin cancelled again for Shirley's wake-up…"

"Oh Christ, no…"

"You doing anything that pays today? In *money*?"

"Sure…" I belch, tasting stale crafty, parking ticket, some gum from a guy in the talkshow line, a couple green oranges I found in the gutter on Franklin.

"You look like you haven't slept since pilot season."

"But I've never felt better. I'm pretty sure I'm levitating."

You can live on love. The shittiest songs you ever heard were right. But only if it's blind love, and only if you're a psychic vampire. Fame is the purest, cleanest form of blind love. It can feed you. Fame alone. In lieu of food, shelter, drugs… well, most drugs.

Jimmy Angel was this teen heartthrob in the 50's, allegedly. He still performs on 2nd and 4th Mondays at this Mexican restaurant across from a bowling alley in Burbank. Dogshit act. Voice like an ice cream headache. Looks like a big, angry baby, or Little Lulu's boyfriend, Iggy (read a newspaper!), with a half-melted duck's ass toupee that slides around on his head when he does his Chuck Berry walk. The dye in his eyebrows runs into his tiny, beady eyes and he forgets where he is, but he keeps the dozen or so regulars riveted. Wanders the San Fernando Valley the rest of the month in his disfigured wig and a one-piece black Dacron jumpsuit with a zipper from left ankle to neck. Bopping. Never stops. Hasn't eaten solid food since 1997, hasn't slept for more than an hour at a time since 2004.

Tell me Jimmy Angel isn't living his life right. Tell me magic doesn't happen in this town.

I've had to take Jimmy's drunken, toothless (love will feed you, but it won't buy you dentures) testimonial to love's magical power at face value, however, because I've never personally felt it. Nobody knows my name. I'm that guy who got beat up for giving out invitations to John Travolta & Tom Cruise's gay wedding out front of the S_____ Celebrity Center. I didn't get sued for that, but the fame from it made my body hair fall out and my scalp flaked off down to the bone. Took a year to grow back. So I know the perils of the wrong kind of fame.

That girl's smile fills my belly with honey-colored light.

"Look, you go entertain Mom, and maybe I can do something about your infantile fixation thing."

"Ew, no. Just find her for me?"

"I'm not a fucking skip trace, dude."

"You know everybody."

"And they let me live in a trailer under a fucking bridge. So don't expect a miracle."

"Thanks, Mimi."

"Get out of here. Shirley's up in twenty minutes."

Mimi has an Uber deliver me over the hill to a cul-de-sac in Toluca Lake. The house would be heartbreakingly familiar to you if you omnivorously consumed sitcom television of a particular era. Smack-dab in a picture-perfect backlot neighborhood with the kind of classic four-bedroom houses working people can only afford to live in on television.

I let myself in the gate on the east side, ignoring the frenzied, snarling barking coming out of the speakers under the eaves. I go down the east side yard and climb the rope ladder behind an Italian cypress hard against the faded, crumbling stucco of the house, up and in the open window of the second story bedroom.

The air tastes like someone left an iron plugged in and turned up until it aerosolized, but it's so cold I can hear goosebumps rising on my skin.

I do more degrading, dehumanizing shit before 9AM than most people do at their last office Xmas party. This is the worst one, because I can't admit to anyone but myself how much I love it.

I disrobe and bag my clothes, unwrap a fresh pair of pajamas from the wardrobe. Where the fuck her manager finds adult footie pajamas, I don't want to know. I pull back the covers on the stubby twin bed shaped like a Formula One racer in the goat-smelling bedroom, lit only by a deserted saltwater aquarium. Some asshole left a battered paperback copy of *Spoiled Rotten* on the nightstand. I throw it in the trashcan with the others. Break an amyl nitrate ampule under my nose, and think of the Pictures.

Commit to the Pictures.

Feel the Feelings.

Burn the Pictures.

I lie there squinting when the door opens and America's favorite forgotten sitcom mom leans in to say, "Wake up, sleepyhead. The dog's got his eye on your waffles."

"Oh, come on, Mom," I moan, "you know Sandy won't eat your cooking." I reach over and push the snooze button on the fake alarm clock on the nightstand. A peal of canned studio audience laughter, circa 1991, shivers the frigid air.

On the bedpost just behind my head, legions of actors have notched their initials while waiting for this gig to be over. The top one was the actor who played the original Chip, the feisty youngest in the Persons household. S.H. was a legendary douchebag, so I guess that's why somebody's always scratching out his initials, and somebody else always puts them back. I add a hashmark next to my well-worn C.P.

I don't stick my finger in her rectum. I don't get her pregnant. She smiles and her breath smells like Virginia Slims and real Vermont maple syrup. Humming *The Persons* theme song, I get up and go to work.

SIX

[CUE: Alphaville, "Afternoons In Utopia"]

From the Pioneer Psylosophy Lectures of Xavier Doderlik, Vol. 1

Why would anyone want to be famous?

It's not a question you hear asked too often in this town, because everybody has the same insanity.

But step outside the drama club lockdown ward for a second and look at it from the outside. What is fame? The blind love of strangers who think they know you, who want to fuck you and climb inside you and tear you apart and pin a scrap of you on their wall at the center of a shrine.

Once, marrying for love was rare, reckless and frowned upon by those with anything to lose or leave behind. Guess who made it not only normal, but made anything less seem a villainous betrayal of the grand design?

I don't think God is Love. I've seen too much shit, and you have, too. But I'll say this... in Hollywood, and thus all around the world, Love is God.

That's all we make. For the sake of all those too lame, too homely, too poor or just too awful to ever know it or feel it for themselves.

And why? Because it takes the love of a lot of strangers to fill a hole in yourself. And what good is that love? You'll do anything to chase it, and crash harder than any junkie when it runs out. And when you have it, what is it? Do they know you better than you know yourself? Hell no, if they like you even a little, they must be fucking *idiots*. So you treat them with contempt and get a difficult rep, and they throw you into the volcano and pick the next sacrifice. Immortality is worthless, the fans of the future will be even bigger idiots than the ones today. And one day it'll all burn and the stars will go out and no one will remember, anyway. So who are you trying to fool?

The damages caused by that love, the mental gymnastics to deserve and endure it, to make bank off it, are more than almost any human being on this planet can withstand. I'm not talking about when someone admires your work––*I love your work, man*––but when you're looking out of the screen into their eyes and they *know* you see them. When they fall in love with you and they make a place for you in the burnt-out holes where their lives are supposed to have a father figure, a big brother, the lovable girl next door, the smoldering ingénue and a multitude of flattering, mythologizing mirrors, then you're plugged into them. They're either feeding you, or they're fattening you up and stockpiling fuel for a bonfire.

Have you ever felt like you were living in a movie, like there was an audience somewhere just on the other side of a wall that felt false, watching and silently laughing at your failures?

That's the closest you've ever gotten to enlightenment. The great ones know this. That's why they're always on, especially when they are completely alone. Because unless you live your life as if it's being taped before a live studio audience who will tweet your every malfunction into the ground, you will crash and burn on the launchpad...

We're not just a religion for tax purposes, but you

won't hear a lot of talk about God, Jesus or the Bible around here, let's get that out of the way. Because we don't pretend like all the other religions. We're more like your space program, and everyone gets to be an astronaut. Everyone who prays to us will ride a rocket to explore the Universe of You.

The God of this world is dead, if he ever was. He died of boredom. You bored Him to death. Sin and evil weren't invented with atheism and doubt. Shit, the threat of Hell never makes anyone behave like they should in the damned Bible! There are plenty of atheists in foxholes, but not a lot in prison, and I'll tell you why. So-called career criminals are powerless to break the law to please themselves or make a living, especially once they've become marked as convicts. Nobody needs God more than a recidivist drug dealer or a pimp.

So, if God can't even make you be good, how can you become great? You have to internalize that there *is* a God that is alive, and this God is watching you all the time. This God counts all your sins, your failings, and sees right through your lies.

He tells you you're no better than anyone else. Why should anyone care about, why should anyone worship, why should anyone live and die for love of, *you?* He tells you to give up your dreams––get high, get married, get a family and a real job. He'll tell you to put all your faith in a god outside and wait for a break, because He wants you to fail.

If it kills me, I'm going to get you to stop listening to Him. I'm going to get you to recognize that He's inside your head, and He wants to punish you for daring to look up from the rut in the road He's dug up for you.

If it's the last thing I do, I'm going to wake you up to the fact that You have a God inside You. And then, if you still want to stick around, we can teach your God a few tricks...

SEVEN

LA IS JUST LIKE JIM THOMPSON (whoever the fuck *he* was) said: *Ten thousand characters, and no people...*

Actors are the least interesting people in the world, but they have the best stories because they do only the interesting parts of the best jobs, the defining moments of other people's lives.

Here's why actors act like actors.

You take any other creative type, they each have their own their particular methods of being unbearable, whether they're given too much or too little praise, but they don't need anyone else to do their thing. To be what they are, they just need to do it.

From the time of the cavemen, any Neanderthal who smeared his shit on a wall could call himself the first artist, until the first critic dashed his brains out with a club when it didn't magically improve the hunting. Some cave-kid bashed a stick against a rock and invented music. A bunch of folks who'd eaten magic mushrooms growing out of the cave compost pile grooved on it and invented dancing. Some cavewoman who wrapped herself in the skin of a dead game animal designed the first fashion trend. But the first actor was just some guy who never shut up and made a big deal out of everything until someone pushed him in front of a charging mastodon, but by then he'd already knocked up half the cave with his bewitching powers of direct eye contact and expressive pouting, so the lamentable gene was perpetuated.

You probably do some sort of art, and statistically, it's safe to assume you probably suck at it. Can't earn more than fleeting moments of joy in your heart and pity from parents and friends, never mind a living. But when you're dead and gone and your body is discovered by neighbors concerned about the smell or far-future alien archaeologists, your work will rise up to proclaim your sadly overlooked magnificence, and all those wasted years and wrecked relationships will retroactively become vital stepping stones of destiny, a watershed moment for the culture and the species as a whole. You don't need anyone's permission to do this. Just write the most smashingly brilliant poem and bury it in the backyard. You can tell yourself and the intern who writes the local obituary page that you were the greatest poet of the age and who knows? Maybe you're right.

Actors are mad because they need not only an audience, but every other creative type and a little financial backing (or a lot), not to mention each other, before they can perform. Out of the context of a script, a cast, an army of technical support and a camera or audience, they're just obnoxious, needy humans. Our art is nothing without an army behind and before us. Until we are cast, we don't even exist. At least that which does not exist has a certain mysterious dignity. But what is more pathetic than trying to exist, and failing?

Even when given permission to exist, we're utterly powerless, the last decision to get made—the action figure the director moves around in front of the camera, the parrot who'll squawk whatever words the writers feed us. Rejected again and again for reasons we never understand, made to feel more expendable than any prop on the set even when we *do* get the gig, an actor's medium is attention, the same stuff every artist craves unto destruction. Condemned to get high on our own supply, we only live in the fleeting gap between ACTION and CUT.

And if being a failed actor is like being the ghost of an abortion, then how much worse, to be a *star*?

An actor only has to convincingly imitate something they drown in every day—people. A star has to be you as you dream yourself, at once a beautiful twisted aspirational package of everything you wish for and despise about yourself, a king-for-a-day demigod you can worship and spy upon and envy and loathe with the jaded embedded intimacy of a lawyer-gossip columnist-celebrity proctologist, a glamorous, empty wicker man you can stuff full of unfulfilled dreams and burn to the ground when it grows old or weak or otherwise betrays you.

And betray you we will, for our gift is empathy, and if we feel and reflect your pain, sooner or later, we'll choke on it and try to use our own words, and you'll turn on us with irate tweets to stick to playing pretend in make-believe-land, and bumper-stickers branding us traitors unworthy of sucking your unsightly rubber truck-nuts.

Worst of all, we'll turn to dust before your eyes and with our gray passing undo all the glamour of media devised to make you forget that someday you, too, are going to die, except nobody will care.

We feel it more deeply than you when great entertainers die. You cry because you'll never get to see them again. We cry because they'll never get to see *us*.

You must give us permission to exist. Without an audience, we are not even ghosts. But without us, you will always and only be yourselves. And we wouldn't trade for a second with the most outwardly content of you out there in the dark for one solitary instant, not for all the titties in Lake Titicaca.

It's difficult to say how long the Shirley gig can run. Sometimes, she gets uncomfortable and hits the panic button and you have thirty seconds to evacuate before she gets tranquilized or freaks and calls the cops. Others, the alarm upstairs goes off and you bow out as gracefully as you can before the next "kid" comes down the stairs to eat his waffles.

The house phone rings. Mom picks up, then shoves it at me and looks at the floor like she's waiting for me to remember my lines.

"I found your friend," Mimi says.

"I'm really sorry," I whisper to Mom. "It's about the big science fair…"

"Oh," she says, eyes scrambling around the room with posthypnotic resolve, trying not to see the strange man in her son's pj's.

"So…" Mimi whistles. "They don't give up their clients, and they were really pushy about getting my name, but I used a prepaid phone and ditched it. Then they called me back. On *my* line."

"And?"

"*And?* I'm fucking scared shitless, idiot! They come back at me with how they've got this pregnant runaway they're shuttling around town and they're calling me because there's a problem with the credit card."

"Why would they call you?"

"Because it's *your* credit card, you fucking moron." She takes a long, steadying bong rip. Her voice is two octaves deeper, but no more calm. "You gave her your credit card?"

"No…" I pat myself down but of course, my red leatherette wallet is in the hip pocket of my jeans, upstairs. "She must've lifted it."

It's a shitty emergency Visa card with a three-hundred buck limit and an interest rate even the loan sharks' union would have serious beef with. She must've taken it when I was having a mystical communion with her unborn child while touching her belly. The nerve of some people…

"They want to talk to you, now. They know where you are. They say you owe them four thousand dollars, and they're coming for you."

I run upstairs and I'm digging through the plastic bags for my clothes when I hear some massive vehicle screech to a stop out front.

An airhorn blares twice.

I grab a bag at random and jump out the window, slide down the ladder and go into the backyard, around a pool dyed the deep, uninhabitable blue of an airplane toilet-bowl. I hop over the fence into the next yard and around an olive-green pool overrun with algae and bullfrogs, and over a brick wall and through a yard where a middle-aged woman hops on a trampoline. Out the sideyard and onto an overgrown lawn, and I'm running at a good clip when the Subaru hatchback jumps the curb and knocks me sideways into a concrete lawn jockey.

This mean librarian who looks like she moonlights as a dominatrix comes round the car pointing a gun at me with one hand, her other perched delicately on her temple, like how they tell actors to signify that they're doing something psychic.

"I know what you're thinking," she says. "You're asking yourself if you can trust me, and I'm using my superior will to force you to believe that you can. *Trust me.*" Mentally, then verbally, she orders me to get up and get in her car.

I act like I can't get up. She screams at me like *I'm* pointing a gun at *her*, making a raygun noise in her throat and her skinny lips disappear when she presses the hand to her temple hard enough that one eye bugs out. I don't know if she's willing me to obey her or just bodily hoisting me off the lawn and levitating me across the parking strip to her car.

I try to resist, but then I remember that people are chasing me, and they have my credit card and I don't even have my own pants, so I open the passenger door. I needed a ride anyway, and if she's not going to charge me…

"I'm sorry," I tell her, as nicely as I can. "I can't fit in there."

It smells like rancid apple juice and cats. A stack of binders, magazines and loose papers sits on the passenger seat, with a Styrofoam wighead under a pith helmet resting on top, like she's made her crap into a dummy to cheat the carpool lanes. A flat of Korean energy drinks and a huge bag of powdered donuts fills the footwell.

"It's fine, just move it into the back," she says.

The backseat is even worse. Cartons of files, more binders, clamshell cases of DVD's, VHS and audio cassettes, and beat-up, outmoded players for all the aforementioned media.

I try to fit, but the seat won't recline and it's practically crushed into the dashboard by the mountain of shit in the back. "I'm sorry, it's really not a big enough car for a kidnapping."

"Trust me," she grits, "it's big enough, you could lose your whole life in here. Don't make me use *this*."

The way she says this makes me finally look at the gun and notice it's not a gun at all. For just a second, it's a plastic toy raygun thing, the kind that spits sparks or pops gunpowder caps, back before cops shot anyone that pointed anything more menacing than a finger at them.

Then it's not even a toy, but a staple remover, which is kind of scary up close, if you're a staple—those wickedly curved steel vampire fangs in that molded plastic grip so like a cobra's head… She points it at me and does the Professor X thing with her hand and the tip of her tongue comes out, white, between her colorless lips.

So I get in.

She throws the Subaru into gear and lays down a patch on the sidewalk. Still clutching the toy raygun/staple remover against the steering wheel. "What did she tell you?"

"She said to have a nice day and to watch out for bullies…"

"*You know who I mean*! You're helping *her*. You're enabling an outed *Heckler*! The more Yuks she gets, the more everything's going to get unfixably fucked!"

She takes the corner hard and screams into the midst of late rush hour traffic, headed for the 101.

I try to tell her I don't know what she's talking about.

"Say it into the mic, then." She sticks this toy microphone into my hand. "Comedy is the truth," she says. "Make me laugh."

She turns onto Cahuenga and the traffic is slammed and we idle next to a bus stop. I'm having a hard time still feeling kidnapped, but she's put a lot of effort into it. "I'm sorry—I still don't know what you want with me."

The microphone buzzes in my hand and it fucking hurts. My fingers spasm but I can't drop the shitty thing even though it keeps shocking me as I cuss it out.

"Did she tell you whose baby she's carrying? DID SHE?"

"No, I mean… this is about… OW, fuck this!" I drop the mic and open the door, but can't quite get my foot into the gutter.

She's pointing the gun at me, mouthing *Zap Zap Zap*. "I don't *need* to use this, you know. It only focuses my motivation, so it does *less* damage. I could just say your name and make up a song about you and give you an embolism, you joke-jacking waste of space!"

Her scream goes up so high and so loud I can't believe it doesn't crack the windshield. I offer her a breath mint. Something in her mouth is deeply rotten. Her sweat smells like pickles, and she's sweating right through her cardinal red double-knit blazer.

"Where is she? I know you fed her energy this morning, I can smell her on you, so don't lie to me—"

I'm starting to get out when we get rear-ended.

All I remember is biting the windshield, and then the three guys in a wool suit pick me up by the collar of my PJ's and drag me to the backseat of the SUV. He circles back to the Subaru to fetch my plastic bag, throws it in my face.

"Hi," says the pregnant girl.

Her unborn child doesn't say shit.

"You said you wanted to help…"

EIGHT

From the Collected Pioneer Psylosophy Lectures of Xavier Doderlik, vol. 6 (Expanded Superdonor Bonus Edition).

DO YOU DESERVE TO BE SUCCESSFUL? Really?

The next time you're trying to convince yourself you deserve to be successful, I want you to go find the tallest building you can get on the roof of, and I want you to climb up on the ledge and walk along it to the corner facing into the wind, and I want you to shout that you deserve your success.

Go ahead, I'll wait... (Audience laughter, inaudible comment) Wear sensible shoes, yes. (More laughter) And don't jump.

Now, my point... I'll bet none of you can do this at the initiate level. You'd be crazy to try it. Why is that? It's just walking in a straight line and not falling over in the face of a breeze. The consequences of failure shouldn't make you flinch one bit, but can you even close your eyes and picture yourself doing it? I'll bet all you see is yourself tumbling off that ledge no matter how wide it is, or you see all that concrete and rebar crumbling underfoot like a soda cracker, the whole world refusing to hold you up. You're not particularly afraid of heights, but just thinking about it makes your heart race.

(Audience noise, someone is violently ill)

It's because you don't trust yourself. You're not afraid of falling, you're afraid of *jumping*. You don't know it consciously, but there's a part of you that only comes out and takes control whenever there's a risk of total failure, of literal or figurative death. And it not only doesn't want you to succeed, it knows you don't even deserve to exist, and most of the time, it is the boss of you.

This part of you believes you are worthless and will sabotage you every time you step out on the ledge. It will take control when you don't even see the ledge, but you'll throw yourself into the void, just the same.

If you step up onto the ledge with me, you're going to have to lose your fear. I'll show you how to do that. I'll show you how to recognize the invisible ledges out there that so-called friends, family, and society will try to lead you out onto, and push you over: drugs, sex, petty emotional validation and even the deathtraps of marriage and parenthood. You'll learn to stand and face the wind and never fear falling from any height.

And you won't just walk that ledge.

You'll dance.

[*From Vol. 13*]

You fucking saps are still here? You wanna hear some fucking success stories? Great... Suck on this.

There're those who talk, and those who walk. You won't hear our people flogging our mastery of our spiritual infotainment software like home shopping merchandise, okay? Our technology *works*.

You look at any player in Hollywood who should've been dead years ago, who still drinks, smokes, carouses and plays like a man half his age, when all his peers are dead and gone. You want to know how he does it?

Get a dog.

It's like that old saying, you want loyalty, get a dog... Harry Truman didn't fucking say it, actually. (That smartass in the front row. I'm not saying another word 'til he's out of here.) It was put in his mouth by a play in 1975, and everybody from Thalberg to Eisner has had it put in his mouth since. But nowhere is it truer than here. If you want a friend in Hollywood, get a dog.

So, you get a dog. And you name it something, but that's not its real name, you make damn sure it knows its *real* name, you give it your name, so it comes when you call your name. And you make damn sure that dog loves you more than life itself.

It's not hard.

You know, they say dogs just manipulate us, they're so cute and servile because it gets them food and shelter. They're just grifters, and we're all suckers. But they need food, and we need some creature too stupid to see how undeserving we are of love. They give us the unconditional love that we need more than food or shelter, and they're sucked into a relationship they can't possibly understand.

You go home and no matter what kind of day you had, you cuddle that dog and you tell it your fears and dreams and you rub its belly like you're making a fucking wish, and you say its name that is your name, and you'll feel a sense of tranquility, of belonging, of deserving great things and greater love. And with that dumb creature in your lap loving you with all its heart, you can overcome your fears, your neuroses, your learning disabilities, your diseases, your deformities, even the degeneration of age and wear and tear from the consequences of your own

CODY GOODFELLOW

shitty choices.

All of it flows out of you as that unconditional love flows in. And guess where it goes?

Yeah.

When Harry Truman was in office, someone kept giving him dogs, but he wouldn't keep one in the office. Reporters made a stink about it... what kind of guy can't even get a dog to like him? But the real reason was, he'd seen how FDR survived the Depression. All the withering criticism, obstruction and hatred from the opposing party, from the nativists, the isolationists and those who wanted to fight WW2 on the Axis side...

All those millions of people wishing him dead or worse, every minute of every day. How'd he get through it? He had a dog.

A secret dog in a closet in the Oval Office, the same one they caught Warren Harding fucking his mistress in... Some weeks in the 1936 re-election campaign, they went through two, three dogs a week. Puppies snuck out of the White House with polio and lung cancer... Struck blind, deaf and hairless, twitching with magical parasites... Stiffening and dying under his hand when he petted them. It made him sick to do it, but if he didn't, he'd die himself in less than a week. The little dogs licked his hands even as he killed them, drank up their own deaths like mother's milk. His shadow became so toxic it killed everything it touched in the Rose Garden, but he lasted almost to the end of the war.

Hoover––now there's a guy who couldn't get a dog to love him––was the one who took the secret and passed it on to the moguls of the great studios. Warner, Goldwyn, Thalberg, Schenck, Selznick... If you want to throw down with the titans, you'd better have a dog in your corner, or you'd better be the rare kind of mutant that nothing and no one in Hollywood can defeat with any kind of passive aggressive pseudoscientific voodoo. You'd better know the final and ultimate secret:

Nothing and no one can stop you if you're immune to love.

NINE

[CUE: Naked City, "The Sicilian Clan"]

"EVIL WOMAN."

She wrinkles her nose adorably. "ELO, still? See, that would be one of those on-the-nose song choices, right there…"

"What song? I'm talking about *you*."

She takes my hand. Hers is hot, sweaty, skin like melted velvet. Sour grape soda breath.

"I thought you were, you know," she says. "Serious… about, you know… *helping*." Her head bowed, she looks out the window. Every bus kiosk is plastered with one-sheets for Disney releases, because their production facilities are right down the street. The films, TV shows, songs, games are all calculated money-extracting machines, so only the advertising shows any real passion. The spaces between the movie ads becomes a brown blur, the empty space between frames, so the posters seem to dance as we pass.

We cross Buena Vista and all the posters flip to Warner properties. "That crazy lady was carrying on like you're pregnant with the Antichrist." She takes her hand away. I try nonchalantly to smell my palm.

"I don't want anything but the truth. I just want to know… for sure. I don't want their money… I'm not a Ps—"

"We don't say," I say, pressing her knee with mine, her large, mildly lopsided bosom with my arm, "*their* name."

"Well, *whatever*… I'm not one of *them*."

I look away and realize I'm still in pajamas. The plastic bag contains a pair of acid-wash bejeweled jeans, an Affliction T-shirt and a green Dickies chore jacket, all sized for a twelve year-old boy. "Well… the nice thing about taking their money is, they have some."

"I'm sorry about that, I just… Sometimes… like… do you ever hear a Voice? Not like the ones schizophrenics hear, telling them they're the messiah or whatever, but like… a guardian angel, you know? It tells you what to do sometimes, and it's almost always right."

I've become the baton in some kind of mental illness relay race. Her belly brushes against my forearm and something inside kicks me. "So where are you from?"

She squints at me, trying to gauge if I can be trusted with her secret. "Wenatchee," she finally says. "It's in Washington. The state, not the capitol…"

"And you came down here because somebody from the, uh… *Them*… put a bun in your oven…"

Shaking her head, waving her hands around to dispel what I said. "I used to be *normal*, okay? Like, I went out and partied with friends and stuff, and I didn't really think about tomorrow, or what I was gonna do with my life… I mean, like…

"This funny older guy, he stopped into the café, and he gave me a stack of quarters to play whatever I thought set the right atmosphere—that's how he said it—and I played all the best songs on the jukebox, and he said I ought to be a music supervisor, that's how I got to thinking about that, but anyway… I still wouldn't have, you know… I hadn't even been to Seattle, but this one time… This one night, it was—"

"About nine months ago, give or take?"

"Smartass." She slaps me, but not hard enough. "I swear I wasn't that high, but this light came down out of the sky when we were parking up in the hills and I went down by the lake to get away from… Anyway, there was this… He was so beautiful… I didn't believe in angels or space aliens, but he was… God damn. I don't need to believe, now… I *know*.

"And he came to me and told me I would be the mother of the new body of God. And he took me to this silver rocket and the Angel took me into the sky and we fucked."

"He raped you?"

"No. I mean… Is it rape if they make you *want* to? I kind of wanted to want to, but it was like… It was fucking awesome, okay? You can't even believe me, and you're right to look at me like that. But I don't care. I'm not trying to start a church. I just need to know what I'm supposed to do next."

I reach out and put my hand on her belly. "I believe you." I close my eyes and listen.

"You heard it too, didn't you?"

I just nod.

She finally smiles for real. "I never used to be really into prayer or fasting, right? But like, right after, I cleaned up my act and I like turned into a nun… And I never asked for anything, you know, you're just supposed to ask for the strength to deal. But I asked for answers, like what is it all about, and I missed my next period.

"And just last week, the voice told me to come to Hollywood and go and confront the, like, the cult? It said they would recognize, and they'd pull their heads out of their asses and do right by me. Its words. But like…"

"Do right about what?"

"About taking back the cult and saving the world, I guess. But everybody on this list is dead or missing, and I don't know what to do next…"

"Wow." My first instinct is to jump out the next time we slow down, but the safety locks are on and she's smiling at me like the angel might have smiled at her, right before he filled her with his holy star-goo.

"OK, so what's the deal with these guys?"

"Deal is," says the pile of guys in the passenger seat, "we are not doing this job for exposure, no. Someone must pay for our time together." He's got the biggest fucking head I've ever seen. Fists like adult human skulls. The rest of him isn't much bigger than a normal pro wrestler, but he could probably headbutt your brains out your asshole. "Your credit card is not good. Branko will stop at bank for cash, or we must go back office, draw up contract."

"Want a breath mint?" He's got a mélange of cherry vape oil, steak tartar and oral smegma cutting through his musky cologne like period blood on a gymnast's leotard. Not like the cologne is doing him any favors, with its weird diesel, musk and citrus combo, like a lawnmower that ran over a raccoon eating a lemon.

Branko shakes his head, unfazed. "Sugar bad for teeth."

I huddle closer to her and whisper so she pushes her ear to my lips, "Why did you hire these creeps?"

"I needed protection. I wrote the Ps—"

"Hey!"

"*Them*… and this crazy bitch tried to send me ovarian cancer in the mail. My Dad opened it and went straight to the ER, so I don't know if he's got cancerous ovaries now, or what…"

My lips tickled by feathery wisps of her hair, notes of vanilla and coconut oil. "I'll protect you."

I reach into my pocket and take out what I took from the crazy librarian's car. I close my eyes.

And I stick it in the driver's ear.

"Don't make me use this."

CODY GOODFELLOW

TEN

[Cue: Quincy Jones, "Boogie Stop Shuffle"]

THEY RAISED ME TO BE A WEAPON.

A holy ninja, a God-warrior. A ruthless cutthroat defender of the gospel, sworn enemy of whatever they pointed me at.

Most of the Bethlehem Children were placed in loving Christian homes and grew up unaware of their remarkable rescue from nonexistence.

But a few were selected to carry on the good work. We were taught to live off the land in the hills and cities, to defend ourselves with extreme prejudice, to kill quietly and without remorse.

They made us weapons, but then something went wrong.

The group was routed and went into the wind with the FBI on their tails in an operation so covert it never made the news. They hypnotized us, or they woke us up, because we'd always been asleep. Forget everything, they told us, until the day we come back for you, and put into your hands a sword of fire.

But I remember glimpses.

I remember crawling in a tunnel of green thorns through an endless backyard blackberry patch with a bucket, looking for rhubarb for a pie.

I remember eating my macaroni or Cream Of Wheat slow because the cook sometimes stirred pebbles or rusty wingnuts into the food to discourage gluttony.

I remember looking up at a hole in the ceiling and seeing

red eyes looking down at me, and praying to them to take me away, because I thought it must be an angel.

 I remember someone telling me nothing is ever yours just because you buy it with money. Nothing is yours until it breaks and you fix it. No place is ever home until you step over blood to get there.

I remember beatings in grade school, in foster homes, and wishing they'd call me or send the postcard with the word on it, the posthypnotic trigger word that would unleash every deadly thing they'd put into me.

I'm still waiting for that Magic Word.

I remember scanning every dictionary I could get my grubby hands on, scanning and silently pronouncing each and every weird, worthless word, thinking any of them, maybe the next one, could make a monster of me.

ELEVEN

PICTURE THE GUN.

Feel the Gun in your left ear.

The driver snaps at Branko so ferociously, a couple vowels actually sneak out. Branko barks back at him, then takes out his phone. "Girl-like boy has no gun. Stop making Ivo nervous."

The girl takes her hand out of mine and knits them over the dome of her belly, whispering to herself with her eyes shut tight.

"It's not a gun, it's a knife." *(Picture the Knife in his left ear.)* "You want to see it, keep watching his right ear."

Feel the knife, Ivo

Ivo feels the knife. We slew across two lanes going into the intersection across from Universal and nearly T-bone an open-topped Hollywood Tour van that honks two bars of "There's No Business like Show Business" as we pass it.

"Just pull over anywhere on the right, by the subway station… How much do we owe you?"

Ivo accelerates and passes our stop. "4500 dollars," Branko says, "not including gratuity. We know you not have. Feel bad for pregnant girl, so if you like us to liquidate woman following at no extra charge…"

In the rearview, the Subaru runs the red light and flashes

its brights furiously, bogged down behind a Hummer stretch limo and a truck towing a trailer loaded with identical orange Dodge Chargers emblazoned with the Confederate flag. Fuck me running, are they remaking *Dukes Of Hazzard* again?

I'm swimming in sweat. My heart is a hamster in a washing machine. At times like this, I ask myself, *What Would Shinobi Honeycutt Do?* And I reach into my wallet and pull out a random page from *Spoiled Rotten* and I draw whatever wisdom I can from the time he tore up a picture of Sinead O'Connor at the Ace Awards and apologized on her behalf to clerical kid-diddlers around the world, or the time he was fired from a Jell-O commercial for attempting to sodomize Bill Cosby with a Pudding Pop—

This isn't getting me anywhere.

Picture cool, turquoise water. Picture a drink with tropical fruit skewered on a tiny umbrella. Picture the pregnant girl with Ryan Gosling's eyes sucking on your toes.

Feel the Feelings.

"Listen, man… Branko? We got off on the wrong foot, maybe. My lady friend gave you the wrong credit card, and I'm light on cash right now, but we will totally square things… but you have to trust me when I say that we're in the service of something larger than ourselves, and that really has to take priority."

His eyebrows go up. "Is big deal?"

"Bigger than your business, or anything anyone else is doing in the greater LA County area today.

"Seriously."

Branko's nodding like it all makes perfect sense to him. *Do go on*, say his eyebrows.

"I've dropped everything I was doing today because this lady is in dire straits and has to find people who can take care of her. You've done a bang-up job keeping her safe from the crazy librarian in the Subaru, but I can take over from here… and as soon as we've done what we need to do, we'll settle our account with whatever interest you captains of industry care to tack on.

"Now, doesn't that sound better than messing up your

afternoon and the interior of this lovely automobile?"

Branko smiles and puts his phone away, checks himself out in the mirror. Nods and says, "You are very good actor."

"Wow, you really think so? Cos' I was trying not to lay it on too thick—"

"No. Was good. All in the eyes, yes? Was, how you say… Sincere. I believed. Ivo?"

Ivo agrees.

Branko takes out a comically small pistol and points it at my left eye. "Is fifteen-caliber bullet. Made for air marshals, for stopping of hijack. Bullet pancake inside target. No exit, very small entry. Please to give knife."

He's making it hard to concentrate on the pictures. The girl is still sitting, whispering into her steepled hands.

In the movies, pulling a gun is like a winning poker hand. Everybody folds, real cool, until they can flip the script. In real life, you can't predict what anyone will do when you point a gun at them. Some people see it and just freak the fuck out, try to grab it or trap it in the guy's pocket and make him shoot himself in the crotch.

I throw myself across the girl, but at the same time, I clamp down on Ivo's ear with the staple remover. He tries to follow his impaled ear between the headrest and the doorpost but gets stuck and the staple remover comes free with his earlobe and a sizable wedge of cartilage trailing from it and blood comes out of his head like a sluice and covers the window and his hands jerk the steering wheel.

Branko leans to grab the wheel but we're over the double yellow line and a wave of mid-level studio jackoffs in power lunch mode come shooting over the Cahuenga Pass in their silver Audis and we're going to hit at least two of them head-on doing about sixty, and only Ivo is wearing his seatbelt.

Still fighting the wheel, Branko points the gun at my face.

The girl grabs my hand, squeezes it hard and screams, "Close your eyes!"

I was going to do that anyway.

Picture me and her all alone on a perfect beach just over the Ventura County line, with a peppy border collie frolicking around us as we introduce our perfect newborn baby to the ocean. Just letting her tiny fucking feet touch the white rough grains of sonofabitch sand and the cocksucking kiss of the goddamned waves…

It's hard to act under this kind of pressure and I want to open my eyes, surely the cars must've hit us by now and Branko must've pulled the trigger and the bullet is probably hovering right in front of my face like an angry hornet, waiting for me to open my eyes and invite it into my brainpan.

And then her hand slips out of mine and grabs my dick.

And we're just *gone*.

CODY GOODFELLOW

TWELVE

A BIG UPSIDE TO THE FOLLOWING EXPLOSIVE high-concept tentpole franchise platform concept is that, if marketed to tweens, it should have carryover into the target's teen years, when most softcore violence toy franchises lose their appeal in the context of girls, drugs and other teenage concerns. Another one is that a motivated producer could dig up a ton of ancillary funding by tying the production to burgeoning legalization campaigns in selected screening markets.

During a routine clinical experiment to produce the most potent strain of cannabis ever smoked, a freak pharmacological accident causes Gary Wimbish, a clean-cut young high school freshman and valued member of his local D.A.R.E. chapter, to get so high that he goes into a trance and hallucinates into existence a sentient, superpowered being.

The HEAD is a living pot-thought, a cosmic superman ever in danger of fading into oblivion with the fickle flickering of Gary's badly damaged short-term memory. While he is incredibly powerful, able to slow, stop or accelerate the flow of time and infiltrate the consciousness of any human mind in close proximity to Gary's brain, he holds the power to save the world, but only so long as Gary stays high enough to remember him.

In the franchise opener's obligatory origin story, Gary freaks out and manifests the Head when confronted by a random urine test at work, and the Head goes on a rampage.

Meanwhile, another experiment subject, Hideo "Bottomless Pit" Sagawa, a regional competitive eating champ, goes from the lab to the state fair and succumbs to berserker munchies during a pie-eating contest, eating his rivals and many of the audience, becoming a rampaging blob of ravenous bowels dragging along a stunted, skinny guy in Nathan's Frankfurters swag.

Meanwhile, the Head has made Gary an outlaw, but the authorities manage to capture him with a pizza spiked with Ritalin and an endless ASVAB test, Gary having become so sober that the Head disintegrates, and the disarmed stoner aspires to convert to Mormonism and join the Air Force. Gary resolves never to touch the devil weed again, until his stoner buds from the pot lab reveal a dark secret.

The experiment that made sub-functional welfare cases of the rest of the group was not about making pot more potent at all. Driven by falling sales with the all-important youth market, the nefarious domestic beer lobby was trying to induce the pot panic that years of scare-marketing propaganda couldn't, by causing a death by marijuana overdose.

But after police, the feds, the National Guard and America's best science-doing-guys fail to stop the Bottomless Pit, one FBI guy who used to be cool in college slips Gary a tray of funny brownies, and the Head is reborn.

The Head busts out of jail and challenges Hideo to a competitive eating contest. As the Head struggles to gobble wieners, Gary causes the Bottomless Pit to greedily consume himself, ripping open an interdimensional portal to the netherworld where all of the food Hideo ate in his long career ended up. To stop a mass of half-digested hot dogs ten times larger than the earth itself from spilling into our universe, the Head bravely sacrifices himself, closing the portal, but leaving Gary bereft, even as he's borne aloft to a medal ceremony with the Jamaican king of the United Nations, who slips Gary a fat joint, causing the Head to emerge to take Gary's medal.

In the sequel, a dastardly pharmaceutical combine has developed legal knockoffs of street drugs and eagerly pushes for their mainstreaming. To help market the new designer drugs, they form a new super crimefighting team, including the Tweakster, a human blur powered by antidepressants, Microdose, capable of disintegrating into billions of monomolecular men, Dr. Acidpus, who has a neon squid for a head; and Ana Bollocks, a female bodybuilder. But the super team is the front for an operation to hook every man, woman and child on a radical new antidepressant, but what even they don't know, is that FUCK THIS SHIT SOMEONE CUT ME A CHECK, ALREADY.

THIRTEEN

[CUES: Carter Burwell, "I Met Doris Blind" from *The Man Who Wasn't There* OST; Don Henley, "Dirty Laundry"]

I OPEN MY EYES AND TRY NOT TO JUMP OUT of my skin. I'm sitting in the back of a stretch limo, and the hand on my crotch is withered and veiny, tendons like leather thongs straining as it inexpertly honks my junk like an old-time automobile horn. Rings on two fingers, gold and platinum inset with blood-red diamonds shaped like a Maltese cross and a backwards swastika.

I brush it away.

"You're right, we shouldn't indulge so soon before the broadcast. I'm just so… look at me… how nervous I am!"

Yes, look at him.

Those creepy hands run over lustrous white dragon-beard candy hair that's the closest you can get, in this century, to a powdered wig. They stop to brush wiry moth-antenna eyebrows into place above the topaz chips of his eyes, twinkling as if always on the edge of joyful tears. His deep laugh lines look surgically etched, while the rest of his face looks sandblasted to a rosy marble shine. A proud, dramatically crooked nose wrinkles in wry amusement at how those hands shake as he takes up a cut crystal decanter and pours out a brimming tumbler of fortified lemonade.

Part country preacher, part gameshow host. If America has a pope, it's this guy. He certainly couldn't get this far on the strength of his lackluster handjob technique.

Which brings up the question of what I'm doing in his limo. I turn down a glass of lemonade and slide over to mess with the window. The keyboard set into the armrest won't make it go down, but the nearly opaque tint fades away so I can see out.

We're moving at a good clip down the 101's carpool lane with a pair of motorcycle cops in front and behind. Traffic is totally gridlocked in the other four lanes, and most of it's on foot. Some people shout and raise their hands up in jerky ecstasy as we pass by, but most just keep shuffling up the highway, oblivious to the dusty, battered cars crawling along all around them, honking, throwing rocks and bottles.

"What's going on out there?"

"Just folks on the move… Someone's finally serious about resettling the Valley, and these people are moving into the old Persian enclaves in Encino. They were all at-risk single folks and families picked out by their local pastors, so maybe starting over will help them straighten out." He winks and slides closer to me, sizing me up like he's starting to wonder if I'm the same guy he was jerking off a few minutes ago. "I used to think it was so vulgar, how those papists had an effigy of Christ on the cross, it was so morbid, and all… I always thought the plain cross itself as a symbol was so much better, but I never realized how severely they missed the point. It's not Christ's cross if he's not on it. It's yours. We all climb up on it, thinking it helps us get closer to Him, but we never let ourselves see how it ends."

"You always need to ask for help with that last nail," I offer helpfully.

He smiles. "Your irreverent sense of humor will be the death of you. I won't always be around to protect you…"

I put my hand on his shoulder. "You're really nervous. Tell me about it. And do you have anything stronger than lemonade?"

He quails under my hand, but then subsides into his white tailored suit. "I'm not afraid of any man, son. I only fear God's judgment. I'm afraid I've waited too long, and this gesture will only stand out as the too-little, too-late effort of a weak, proud man."

He knocks back the last of his lemonade and tosses the tumbler on the floor. "Son," he says, "do you know why Sodom and Gomorrah were destroyed?"

I shrug. "Because of all the Gomorromy?"

He chuckles. "Oh, they engaged in the sins of the flesh, as men everywhere always have, but it was their arrogance that did them in.

"They built those cities on the backs of the poor and they exalted themselves above all others, and made of their cities graven images of God's creation, and called them the world. They led the people away from the Lord of Hosts, and into the worship of their pleasures, to make false idols of themselves.

"That's why we had to burn down Hollywood. But that's why we had to rebuild here, as well, why the new capitol can't be in Tennessee or Virginia, like the rest of the leadership council wanted."

I don't ask him what the fuck he's talking about. I look.

We're going down the 101 through Cahuenga Pass. The Hollywood Hills are black as coal, and barren of all life. Where the sign once stood atop Mount Lee, a chrome cross so fucking big, they could nail that giant Jesus statue in Rio to it looms like a sword buried in a blackened corpse.

"I used to think I was going to live in outer space when I grew up," he says. "All of us did. Nobody wanted to be a doctor or a fireman or a cowboy anymore, we all wanted to fly rocketships. After we saw *Star Wars* and *2001*—I couldn't ever stay awake till the end, but still—we were spoiled for this world. Space was the new frontier, and movies and TV made us believe it would be like the Old West all over again, with space-cowboys, space-Indians and wagon trains to the stars. It was dangerous and far away, but we'd get there, and we'd have adventures."

The way he says the names of those movies—with a creepy Rosebud kind of nostalgic longing—makes me realize just how deeply fucked this place was, long before I was born. He misreads the look on my face.

CODY GOODFELLOW

"Don't look so shocked. I saw the movies—we all did. Oh, you should have seen them… They were wonderful in the old days, so wondrous you didn't even feel them rotting your soul. And decent, mostly. Wholesome.

"Problem was, people got so they thought they knew what war was like, without ever setting foot on a battlefield. They thought they knew what the whole world was like, without ever getting off their butts. And they thought they knew what God was like, without ever going to church.

"And the stars… The people who acted in them were so beautiful, so talented, you'd go see them in a different movie every month and you recognized them, but you loved them all so much, you didn't care. They were like family, and more than family. They were what we wanted to be, what we wanted others to be, so we stopped seeing each other as anything but ugly, fat failures.

"Sure, they sinned and cheated and lied and stole out here, but it wasn't that. It was what they did right. They made worlds we loved so much we let God's creation go to rot, and the worse things got, the more desperately we tried to live in those false worlds, worshipping those false idols.

"That's why they had to go. They were false gods bearing false witness, and nearly led us all off a cliff. If that bunch of born-again Pentagon generals hadn't decided to serve a higher power than their callow, sinful president, you might have grown up in a very different world."

We pass under a bridge with a dozen hooded people hanging from the railing. A couple rocks bounce off the roof. "Damned Catholic militias are getting bolder," the old man says. "I tell everyone who'll listen public executions don't deter anybody… far from it… but if anyone still listened to *me*…"

He puts his hand on my knee. I let him.

We exit on Vine and go south past the old Capitol tower, which someone has dipped in cream paint and covered in kitschy angel statues. It's now headquarters to the Joyous Noise Music Group.

"Some people thought we went too far with the censorship

laws. It wasn't enough to outlaw the violence, the sex, the blasphemy and obscenity, the glorified vice and such... We were bound to stop the lies, so that's what we did. *Any* fictitious entertainment not taken strictly from the Gospels is anathema, an offense in the sight of God. Thou shalt not bear false witness. Simple as that.

"Well, I don't have to tell you that didn't turn out so well. Not ten years go by, and we're bogged down in the same mire of sin and idolatry we came to cleanse. We still have stars flaunting their sinful bodies, even if nobody knows their names. Ladies still close their eyes and picture Samson from last summer's biblical epic instead of their husbands. Men still curse their wives for not having lips and hips like Salome or Mary Magdalene.

"I'm going to call for us to look at ourselves and go back to the intent of the law, and stop making movies altogether. But what would be enough? If we only used animation or if we rolled it back to radio, the voice actors would become idols, and older children would abuse themselves to the Song of Solomon. The only book they know is the Bible, and less than half can quote from it proper, and even they can't read it.

"I look at the world we saved and wonder if we didn't just fail a test. If we weren't supposed to just grin and bear it and wait for the goddamned Rapture."

I pat him on the shoulder and accept a glass of lemonade. I take a sip. It's mostly vodka.

The limo pulls into a parking lot behind a TV soundstage off Melrose. The old man sees the people outside and says, "Oh, shit..."

The door flies open. A woman with her hair pulled into platinum minarets, wearing a white gown with a cross around her neck you could crucify Lassie on, leans into the limo. "Come on out. Nobody can see you. Your catamite is going to be fine."

"God will not be mocked by your blasphemy," my old man says.

"Zip up your dick, Lester," she hisses. She passes me a note and says, "Take this to the control room. Tell them Brother Llary will be delivering tonight's address, and then wait there."

I take the paper from her. The air is so smoggy, my eyes and

CODY GOODFELLOW

sinuses sizzle in my face. I start to cross the parking lot through two rows of armed guards with mirrored shades and earpieces and assault rifles before I look back.

The old man wails something and the guards climb in to drag him out by his feet.

A guard holds the studio door open for me. I go inside and walk down the hall and this harried looking bald guy with a headset looks at my note and tells me to go out in the lobby, where there're even more guards and a bunch of people on their knees with hoods on waiting to be loaded into the trashtruck parked out front, and I don't want to go and he pushes me through the doors.

I'm screaming *Feel the Pictures* with my eyes closed and hands are grabbing me and kids wailing in my face security guards drag me kicking screaming into the lobby of a Nickelodeon game show taping and I'm trying to get away but I can't get any traction on the polished concrete floor in my footie pajamas.

FOURTEEN

[Cues: In The Nursery, "Blind Me"; Michael Brook, "Andean"; The Prodigy, "Climbatize"]

IN SPITE OF THE GENERAL MISPERCEPTION THAT Hollywood is a coherent vehicle for promulgating secular humanism and anal sex, producers will produce anything and actors will say anything, to get paid and be loved, respectively. Actors skew liberal because our art is empathy and imitation. We naturally put ourselves in other people's shoes, and we get the most mileage out of other underdogs, outsiders and freaks. But if we were sincerely liberal, we all would've voted for *Hidden Fences* instead of *La-La Land*, but nobody can resist a flattering mirror.

Studios wrack their brains trying to duplicate the success of shit like Harry Potter, but it's not the magical school bullshit or the needlessly circuitous, overexposed plots or the brutal abuse of adverbs that keeps the piglets sucking that tit.

It's the endless procession of adults and godlike personages who remind the juvenile protag how terribly brave and vitally important they are to the saving of all things from some silly evil shit that makes all the grownups pee with helpless terror.

Everybody's doing YA dystopia franchises that drive home the message that adulthood = fascism. But they're still not giving people what they really want. Which, if what I see of Facebook over other bus and subway riders' shoulders is any indication, is outrage.

So, depending on how the election goes this year, here are two modest proposals for a blockbuster YA series. I hear these things all start out as books, so if anyone wants to take this concept and run with it, we can figure out the split on the back-end when someone options it.

BLUE PROPOSAL

Life is so idyllic and perfect in Suburbistan that the schools have decided to stop teaching history, because it makes kids anxious and depressed in an otherwise perfect world. And what need is there to reflect on the troubling past, when the present offers a world without want, poverty or suffering?

Dad designs skyscrapers and golfs and hunts with his buddies from the country club; Mom gets bombed with her friends and writes her saucy column for a trendy magazine, while the kids ride horses, swim, sunbathe and indulge in the pleasures of a bucolic maze of cul-de-sacs, pocket parks, shopping malls and robot bandstands. Goats eat the grass and mice and pigs eat the trash, so nobody has to mow or clean. Dogs and cats kill the goats and pigs, and cats kill the mice, and all share the spoils with their rightful master, Man.

So the world has always have been, and so might it be forever, if Kyt, a bright-eyed girl-next-door just a bit kinder and prettier than her peers, did not step in to rescue a parrot about to be executed for the crime of blasphemy. It was calling its master a Racist, which offended everyone gravely, though they had no idea what it actually meant.

The grateful parrot reveals that it knows much more than a few stock phrases like, "Nice swing, boss!" and "Give it to her good, sir!" It knows the secret history of Suburbistan.

Once, their idyllic utopia was part of a much larger, angrier nation, before an ecological holocaust destroyed all the crops, turning the farms to putting greens and driving ranges and all the forests into fashion magazines, and all the people who didn't like golf or upscale ladies' opinions on casualwear were mutated and devolved into goats and pigs and dogs and cats and some particularly sad remnants became parrots who rode their masters' shoulders, assuring them they were the pinnacle of creation.

Kyt shares these horrible secrets with some of her friends, who begin making investigations of their own. Tym learns that the computer that renders Dad's sloppy drawings of dicks and boobs into elegant and sturdy office and tower residence properties is really just a brain in a jar, cloned from a long-extinct race that Dad's ancestors enslaved as accountants and engineers. And Mom's computer that converts her moans of vapid ecstasy into insightful tips for how to please your man and reviews of the Versace spring line was merely another brain bred for its lurid imagination and trend-calculating skills, while her vibrator is really the last remnant of another sub-race renowned for its superior cocksmanship.

Nothing they have, wear, eat or use is not derived from the flesh, bone and misery of their ancestors' ethnically unfortunate neighbors. Following the parrot's instructions, they plant his birdseed and smoke the resulting crops, gaining much forbidden knowledge, as well as a new appreciation for rhythm-based music and competitive sports. The kids rise up against their parents, who in turn reveal to them that they aren't children at all, and so of no emotional value to those they've loved and learned from all their short, soft lives. They're clones, spare parts grown to prolong the lives of the few healthy but sterile adults valuable to the survival of Suburbistan.

By the climax of Part 1, the kids have successfully rebelled against their parents but granted them mercy, if they'll only let them leave Suburbistan. The parents relent, but are exterminated by the central authority, which pursues the young freedom fighters, who sow the parrot's seeds far and wide and teach the animals to make sick beats and raps about being free and having unprotected sex and yielding free, high-as-fuck warrior babies to take up the struggle against the monstrous dominators.

CODY GOODFELLOW

Painting their faces to make themselves look like animals and busting sick barnyard animal raps, the teenagers turn the tables on the highest of the high powers of Suburbistan and finally overthrow the flabby, incompetent inheritors of their despoiled planet. As the credits roll, our heroic race-traitor teens drop trou and commence returning the world to its natural balance the only way they know how, by copulating with the degraded races to bring their children's children's children back to full humanity.

My original ending had our heroine wake up from a climactic bestiality encounter to find herself in a virtual reality rig, awakening from a critical pre-graduation standardized test of her faculties and finding herself flunking out for having shown no racial sensitivity, and for having failed to assimilate into the simulated culture of extinct *Homo sapiens caucasoidus*.

But a marketing guy I met at El Coyote at closing time who let me live in his pool house until his wife came back and had some guys throw me over the fence and down the canyon where I rolled and tumbled through sixty kinds of exotic invasive scrub brush to end up with a broken nose washing dishes at Coney's Hot Dogs on Ventura told me that a far better strategy would be to end with the heroine on top and reboot the franchise every twelve years with the previous heroine recast as the villain.

RED PROPOSAL

This one would be a lot cheaper to make than the blue pitch, admittedly. While the former would be a thirty-four episode miniseries on Netflix and Amazon, this one would be a ninety-minute feature shot for under a million, but you'd need to spend ten million on an ad campaign to convince churchgoing Americans that Hollywood wants the movie to fail, so they'll bus their suckers out to see it en masse.

Joan Farkis is an ordinary American heartland teen with a good job at her local Walmart in exurban Arkansas, but she's luckier than most of her friends, who are destitute since the wheat and corn crops abruptly moved down to Mexico due to ecoterrorist global cooling, and resettlement of the entire populations of Bangladesh, Palestine and the Netherlands on the old family farms have left many with no option but to beg refugees for spare care packages.

Worst of all, when a UN Refugee Monitor Patrol ransacks the store, Joan's best friend Tammy uses the toilet in the employee washroom after a Pakistani stormtrooper laden with looted Hot Pockets urinated on the seat, and she gets pregnant.

In a panic, Tammy begs Joan to take her to the big city in the next state, where abortion is provided on-demand at walk-up vending machines, and Joan, a loyal if naïve friend, agrees to take her.

But at the very moment Joan is about to put the coins in the abortion machine, an ANGEL appears to her and tells her that the Lord is sick and tired of the evils of the world, most especially the constant industrialized sacrifice of innocent unborn babies; but rather than drown the world again, He's just thinking of throwing a Lana Del Rey CD on repeat, gobbling a bottle of OxyContin and slitting His wrists in the bathtub.

Joan pleads with the angel to pick someone else; she's only one ordinary home-schooled girl with a loaded rifle rack and a wall full of trophies from several statewide church-sponsored sharpshooting competitions. (She would've gone to the Olympics, but she abstained when the Committee couldn't guarantee she wouldn't have to compete on a Sunday.)

At the angel's urging, Joan blows away the abortion machine. But while even the godforsaken state she's in recognizes both concealed-carry and stand-your-ground laws, Joan's loud public prayer violates a host of little-known federal statutes, and Joan and her pregnant friend are on the run.

At first, Joan is crushed by her responsibility… but soon, her act of faith mobilizes an army of freckled-faced kids who rise up against the abortion machines, which she soon discovers provide stem cells for the rejuvenation of unholy coastal

CODY GOODFELLOW

elites and liberal celebrities. And just as the Philistine refugee hordes bearing a brazen idol of Dagon storm the industrial cattle feedlot where Joan midwifes as Tammy gives birth to the Messiah, God reluctantly decides not to kill Himself, but instead raises the sea levels to wipe out half the US population in the coastal urban areas.

But who're we kidding? No matter what color the whores' underpants are, they'll be dancing to the same tune. Hardworking Americans who're one pink slip away from a workplace massacre insist that government should be run like the business they dream of purging in fire and blood. They're sick and tired of lying down with whores, and aspire to get raw-dogged by the pimps.

And to that end, I've whipped up the following can't-miss mass-appeal dystopian tentpole pitch. You're welcome, Hollywood...

A commuter train from Boston to New York, filled with people reading on their phones, Kindles, laptops, etc. But then one kid, reading an attachment he's been sent, loses control of his phone. It blinks a hypnotic pattern as cables shoot out of it to link with the laptop of the guy sitting next to him. That laptop shoots out cables, linking and fusing with phones, e-readers, every wireless, enabled device. Then they link together to form a gigantic killing machine that begins mowing down the helpless commuters, moving from car to car, absorbing all devices until it becomes large enough to derail the train, then stride across the landscape wielding the train-cars like a pair of nunchaku...

ONE WEEK EARLIER...

All his life, Kevin has dreamed of being a great Hollywood screenwriter, but as the most bookishly attractive, sensitive teen in a backwater flyover town, he knows he'll have to put aside his dreams to help keep his family's struggling used bookstore afloat. But in his heart, he believes that one more high-concept superhero-sci-fi-action potboiler can change the world.

As a last heroic act of faith, he writes his magnum opus,

a ten-page synopsis of his pitch for a sprawling epic about a young man in a small town who acquires superpowers to fight zombies, giant robots and kaiju monsters as the vanguard of an alien invasion, but soon realizes that an evil artificial intelligence has corrupted our reality, leaving us all trapped in an evil dream.

Hardly *The Sun Also Rises* or even *The Power Rangers*, but it's got heart, grit and sincerity. It not only finds a way to make tired summer box-office clichés fresh again, it somehow penetrates to the heart of these well-worn commercial myths and shows us why we keep revisiting them.

Kevin is insecure about his own talents, but he impulsively sends it to Claire, a way-out-of-his-league college-bound literary snob who refuses to read his "childish escapist nonsense," and tells him she only dates poets, because only poetry can change the world. In a fit of pique, Kevin sends the pitch to his best friend, Seth.

A clownishly horny comedic relief wing-man who deflects his friend's toxic narcissism with his far broader desperation, Seth clerks at the video rental shop next door. He believes in Kevin, far more than Kevin believes in himself. He thinks his friend's dreams are their ticket to fame and fortune, and maybe someday getting Seth laid. So Seth posts his friend's pitch online, with some minor adjustments: using blockbuster intellectual properties in place of Kevin's own characters (if Warner Brothers produces, then DCU; if Disney, then Marvel/Star Wars; if Sony, then Spider Man/Smurfs) to get his friend's work "noticed."

And then the murders begin…

In a multiplex orgy between *The Ring*, *The Matrix*, *Walking Dead* and *Transformers* franchises, some nefarious force employs every summer blockbuster overkill cliché in the book to crush anyone who reads Kevin's pitch, in fact, to stop anyone reading ever again.

The frightened townspeople riot and try to burn down the family bookstore. Nefarious android lawyers in a fleet of black Escalades soon turn up at the little white farmhouse in the cornfield where Kevin, Claire and Seth hole up with Kevin's English teacher, a blacklisted Oscar-winning screenwriter who deplores everything written since Henry Miller died, but who dies helping the boys realize their dream of saving humanity by hitting the road for Hollywood.

After a pulse-pounding parade of set-pieces of ever-escalating mass destruction, Kevin, Claire and Seth cross a devastated America to confront the enemy, an artificial intelligence responsible for generating all of the major studio's topline cinematic and television content. Because the stakes at the box office have become so very high that no human mind can be trusted to generate satisfactory returns, the AI took over all studio operations and began driving coherent market growth from one summer to the next. When news divisions failed to earn out, it began programming the news, political policy, religion, every aspect of out cultural lives, keeping the whole wired audience in a guided dream.

And everything was going swimmingly, until Kevin's heartfelt scenario appropriated its zealously protected brandeds to tell a story it could never conceive of, because it lacks heart. Presented with the fatal logical fallacy that humans want original entertainment but fail to support it at the box office, the studio AI has degenerated into the kind of insanity a bone fide brain surgeon would feel, running the grill at *Jack In The Box*. The studio demands that box office returns increase every year. The audience grows increasingly difficult to entertain, while past box office receipts show humans are most entertained by the end of the world. ERGO, the AI is determined to end the world and make it as marketably entertaining as possible.

After Seth sacrifices himself so Kevin can get inside the insane AI's never-ending party at its split-level ranch-style cyber-fortress inside the Hollywood sign, Kevin must engage in a duel of high-concept scenario pitches with the AI to save humanity from being destroyed by its own nightmares.

At this moment of truth, he doubts himself. He grew up reading the same generic triumphalist edgelord bullshit everybody else did. How could he possibly outwit a diabolical artificial intelligence programmed to maximally exploit the world's most marketable intellectual properties?

When he needs to hear it most, Claire breaks down and admits to Kevin that comic books and genre entertainment are the closest our insane, suicidal species will ever come again, to true poetry. They sort of convincingly kiss just before the AI incinerates her to reestablish that he's a badass.

Kevin stumps the AI by presenting it with a pitch for a feature with zero budget, no SFX, no bankable leads and no pre-existing IP entanglements—a black and white found-footage comedy about two idiots working as clerks who get lost in a haunted forest. The AI calculates potential risk against revenues and has a cyber-seizure, shuts down everybody's phones, the Internet and all but three TV channels.

Hollywood is ruined, reduced to holding garage sales of priceless memorabilia and offering to perform classic movie monologues for passersby on the street. Kevin hitchhikes home to find a line around the block at the family bookshop, and girls throwing their panties on a freshly erected statue of his fat, sweaty friend Seth in the town square.

Then Kevin goes into the back and boots up his old Macbook running non-pirated MS Office and starts to write.

An annoying software agent window pops up and says, "It Looks Like You're Trying To Remake The World... Would You Like Help?"

It's the AI. Still plugged into and controlling every aspect of reality, the AI erases the entire world as soon as Kevin opens a new, blank page, and when he starts to type, the world reinvents itself as an edgelord douche-utopia where everyone can fly and wears their underwear outside their pants, and everyone who isn't an edgelord is a zombie you can reduce to squeezy gibs without getting in trouble. Kevin types furiously and then sits back for a moment, looking at a doodle he once did of himself flying with Claire in his arms, like Lois Lane. He thinks about that kiss, about what she said to him just before she was cremated to give him motivation...

Kevin types a couple more lines, then hits THE END.

There's a knock at the door. Before he can answer it, a resurrected Seth comes waddling in, draped in the panties of every girl in town.

They go outside. A reunited Limp Bizkit rap-rocks the shit out of Smashmouth's "All-Star," and everybody in town is getting down. It's raining Mountain Dew, and the dying corn crop is now yielding a bumper crop of Swedish bikini babes.

The two bros look over the world they've made, and they high-five, grow capes and, arm in arm, fly into the setting sun…

FIFTEEN

[CUES: Ray Charles, "Busted"; Lord Creator, "Big Bamboo"; Sleigh Bells, "Kids"]

I HATE THAT FEELING… THE BEAVER FEELING.

Vicarious guilt. It started on afternoon reruns from a simpler time. Maybe you're not of an age when even the biggest cities only had three or four broadcast TV channels, and children with no friends were hostage every afternoon to the most toxic of syndicated sludge, back when imbecilic moralists still tried to use television to mold behavior, where Lucy and Ricky slept in separate beds because they had no secondary sexual characteristics and Little Ricky was a homunculus, not because they secretly despised each other.

The worst offender was *Leave It To Beaver*—Goofus with no Gallant, a feeb fuckup who found a new way every day to heap shame and ignominy upon his otherwise exemplary home long before drugs or masturbation were invented. And every day, when he dragged Whitey or Larry Mondello into his hapless fuckupery, he also dragged you and me, and tarred us with po-faced, secondhand guilt.

It was a long time before I realized that nagging pinch in my soul, when I hurt someone or took something that wasn't mine, was not genuine guilt, but just that Beaver feeling, that bedwetting dipshit's ghost in the back of my mind, and not anything I was capable of feeling on my own, thank god.

Lester, I think I hear my Mom calling—

So I'm running for the Hollywood transit center and just as I jump on the escalator, this kid with his Ed Hardy hoodie cinched up Unabomber-style comes running up and kicks me in the junk so I go tumbling down the razor-edged staircase with both hands clenched between my thighs.

I don't, as a rule, do my own stunts, but I've been thrown down enough staircases to know how to break my fall. I'm still lying on the grill at the bottom when he catches up to me and pats me down.

"Sorry, man," he says, "thought you were somebody else." He needs a place to burn a joint right now and he'll smoke me out if we can go to my car.

"I don't have a car, Llary."

The kid pulls a can of pepper spray. "How'd you know my fucking name? ANSWER ME! Who do you work for?"

I try to remind him I'm his best friend.

Llary looks just shy of eleven, or ten and three-quarters, as he puts it when he's working. He has passed for almost-eleven for over thirty years, plying his trade with pedophiles, pederasts, catamites, saprophytes, gropers, molesters and every non-union casting director in the Southland. He's got some kind of glandular problem he tells everyone he got from hormone treatments, back when he was thirteen, and the *Snowed In* film franchise that made him a star at age six finally went bust.

Under the hoodie, Llary's made up like an acrobat in a Chinese opera, so I know he's been working, but it's not all servicing defrocked bishops for our busy little man. For a reasonable kickback, the management at the Hollywood Wax Museum lets him pose in his trademark *Snowed In* snowsuit with tourists for pictures for cash in the café-gift shop, where he also lifts wallets, phones, cameras, whatever. If the rubes realize they got picked, the tweaker carnies working the door buzz him so he rolls out waxwork Llary and hides in his "treehouse" in the engine room from *Hunt For Red October*. He gets antsy every time a new submarine movie comes out, fearful it'll be a big enough hit they'll update and he'll have to move, but

Black Sea bombed last season, so he's safe for now.

We ditch the subway and hoof it east on Hollywood until we come to the Arabian Nights Inn, out near Western, across from United Fruitcake Outlet.

A lot of these places put up phony photos on their websites, trading on flyover state rubes desperate to hit Universal Studios and the incredibly disappointing Hollywood sign and too lazy to double-check the place on Yelp or Google Street View, so they'll pay over a hundred bucks a night to lie awake in a dump with fist-holes in the walls and stains on the beds that you pray are only shit.

The guy who ran the Arabian Nights really hated the owner of the Ziggurat Arms next door. So he poisoned his rival's lobby coffee, which killed the owner and three guests, and offed himself in the bridal suite before the cops could arrest him. The victim's family sued and won the Arabian Nights, so they knocked out the wall between the manager's offices and now, a handful of kids who don't speak English try to run both doomed motels from the windowless dungeon of their studio apartment.

One of the amenities I never bring up in my many paid favorable Yelp reviews is the ease with which the locks can be picked. We go into a room with passable luggage and I change into a baggy pair of black jeans with a white belt, a photoprint NASCAR dress-shirt and bolo tie, and a pair of white alligator loafers, while Llary swipes a pair of cargo shorts and a rhinestone-encrusted Ed Hardy wifebeater.

The dumb fuck left his phone charging in the bathroom, so while we get high, we stuff his inbox full of pics of closeups of Llary's wang with copious notes from a secret admirer. Then I forward one to his wife's Facebook, right above a stove-hot selfie of the happy couple enjoying a twenty-dollar margarita at Citywalk.

I keep trying to remember to tell him about the girl and the Transnistrian bodyguards and the leap into a parallel universe, but I keep ending up pitching him my idea for a sitcom that he should get attached to.

He waits until I forget what I was saying again. "So dude, this one time, I think was the second season Christmas party... I smoked some DMT with the teamsters, and I had this flash, like... It was realer than this, or anything before or since. *Real*, motherfucker!"

"I believe you. Damn."

"But it was weird... I was like on this throne and like all these fucking fly bitches with machineguns, like Victoria's Secret-quality and shit, and they were all knocked up and I knew they were all my ho's. And they were like fanatics, right, like they'd do anything for me...

"And they came to me and told me that the plague we'd sown among the nonbelievers had wiped out all of Europe and Asia and Africa, and it was spreading across America like a wildfire, and all the surviving fly bitches were gonna get on my shit to repopulate the earth... and then I came out of it.

"I did a ton of that shit but it never came back, but like... sometimes, I'll go around a corner or wake up from a nap and, like things'll be kinda different, like somebody else is on the money, and I'm the head of this big church, and I'm on TV and almost nobody gets to be on TV unless they're holy and I'm one of the holiest, I'm on TV all the fucking time... and then I blink, and it fucking goes away. I've tried everything, man. I don't believe it's the fucking drugs. It's out there, if I can just fucking find it before I grow up too old to see it."

I almost show him the crumpled note in my pocket. "Jesus Christ, superstar. You should get that looked at. Real talk."

"Fuck you."

"Straight up, you're losing your last nut, Secret Squirrel."

"Fuck you sideways." Llary sulks for a minute, face a puckered hole, thinking about crack. Peels off his wig and wrings the sweat out, then digs around in his fanny pack and holds up two fresh ones. "Which do you think?"

I point at the straight blond bowl. "Definitely the Cousin Oliver, man... definitely."

He looks at the kinky red one and tosses it in the tourist's suitcase. "You're right, nobody wants to party with Danny

Partridge anymore." Reaches for the remote, but of course, it's bolted to the nightstand. "Mistrustful Procrustean assholes," he snarls at the remote. Animal noises, trying to rip it off.

A conversational void yawns between us, so before he can suggest we make a sex tape, it just slips out. "D'you ever think if it's wrong, what you do?"

Llary looks up, miffed. "Why should I? Prostitution should be legal. Sex is nine-tenths fantasy, anyway. If they want to believe, let them believe. I'm having some of the best sex of my entire life. Is it wrong to fuck a little person and fantasize about a child? Maybe for them, but they pay five to ten times as much until they find out I'm older than they are, and then they *really* dig deep, if they don't want the world to know. So, yeah, it's not *Snowed In IV*, but it's still showbiz."

"That's what I mean, though. Show business. It's like... worse than whoring. I'm starting to wonder if we're not just wasting our lives lying to people, lying to ourselves. Like maybe the whole thing is... wrong."

"Just now seeing that?" He peels a soiled rubber glove off the underside of his pillow. It's the same livid, day-glo fuck-you-eyes lime green that everything comes in, this year. "Hey, why the fuck is everything this awful shade of green, now? It's like shit came out of a meteor, or something..."

"Blame the Seahawks," I say.

He looks at me mistrustfully. "What the fuck are the Seahawks?"

"Forget it."

"No, seriously... Is it a boy band? Cos that name sucks worse than this color."

"Just please turn the TV on, please."

Llary finally finds the ON button, shaking his head like my vice puts his to shame. "Whores just give you the clap. *This* shit should be illegal. It gives you *hope*."

The KCAL 9 midday anchor is doing the weather report on a waterslide with her dog. The SCAN button sticks and the TV barrel rolls through its savagely amputated basic cable package.

We're laughing at it when I sit up and yell at him to make it stop.

Gameshow–talkshow-soapopera-talkshow-infomercial-talkshow-THAT

The picture jumps and twitches, oddly leached of color. A reporter standing in front of the gates of the Hollywood Psylosophy Center tries to shout over bullhorns and a loud PA blasting distorted music. Everybody's stoked because Psylosophy is pushing to get tax-free status as a legitimate religion.

I ask, "Where the fuck is this?"

"I don't know, but it's got to be a joke. There's no Psylosophy Center in Hollywood, or anywhere else. You know what the real deal with those assholes is…"

"Shut up, Llary!"

Straining to pick out the bassline through the squelched PA and crummy TV speaker. It's "Jungle" by ELO.

A woman stands behind the gates, waving to the camera over the reporter's shoulder like stupid people in crowds always do on local news remotes. When the reporter is shoved out of frame by running protestors, the camera autofocuses on the waving hand.

It's *her.*

Live feed.

My pregnant girl's waving at the camera. Waving at me. Behind her stands the lady with the raygun.

And that's when somebody kicks in the door.

A big guy and a bigger guy come in, wearing cheapo luchador masks. Llary springs off the bed and locks himself in the bathroom, but they don't go after him, they come right at me.

The big one shouts, "Girl-like boy!"

Screaming that I don't have their money, I leap from the bed and grab for the light fixture, swinging for a delirious split-second over their heads, until it snaps. I flying-tackle the bigger guy. He basket-catches me and crushes me in a sleeper hold.

An elastic hood snugs over my head and they drag me out the door and down the stairs and across the motel parking lot and toss me into the back of a van like roadkill.

SIXTEEN
[Cue: Hot Butter, "Skokian"]

THIS WAS MY BEST PITCH FOR A SITCOM.

THE SLOTTER HOUSE

Gerald Slotter has always worked hard at the local meatpacking plant to provide for his wife and three kids, so naturally, he spares little pity on those less fortunate. *Get A Job*, he tells the homeless panhandler he passes on the way into what turns out to be his last day at work.

Because there's no more meat to pack.

A combination of environmental and economic and ethical factors have made it unfeasible to package and sell animal meat products anymore. Gerald takes his pink slip home, thinking it can't get any worse… but then it does.

See, the straight-talking politicians Gerald has always trusted to protect his way of life have responded to the looming economic crisis the only way the corporate world will allow… by bringing back debtor's prisons and reclassifying debt-ridden masses as property, to be dispensed with by their creditors in any way they see fit.

In less than a day, the Slotters lose their cars, house and Jet Skis, but the bank isn't so hard-hearted as to turn them out on the street.

As property of the bank, the Slotters are packed onto a bus, issued their new uniforms and ushered into their new home…

At the old slaughterhouse.

Dressed in cow costumes (so as not to upset passing motorists), the Slotter family joins thousands of other shiftless, poor and unlucky Americans in the stock pens, waiting to be used for hideous scientific experiments or simply whisked up the ramp to the killing floor.

With the air hammer just a pink slip away, Gerald and his family will have to connive, cheat and weasel their way through every hilarious episode as they push neighbors, friends and loved ones ahead of them on the conveyor belt to America's dinnertable.

SEVENTEEN

[CUES: Brad Fiedel, "SWAT Team Attacks" from *Terminator 2* OST; FEAR, "Let's Have A War"; The Pogues, "Dirty Old Town"]

"IS EASY MONEY," BRANKO SAYS, "IF YOU GET NOT killed…" Then he thinks about it. "I mean… Is easy money either way for *us*, but for *you*… even if you, you know, survive… then get nothing, sure, but we are *even*… so still win-win."

This is supposed to make me feel better, so I can focus on the job at hand, which, as jobs go, is pretty simple: *Run for your life.*

I try to explain to them that I don't even know that pregnant chick, and don't see how it's fair that I should have to pick up her debt, and if they'll call my agent, we can work something out, and that's when they start giggling—Branko first, then Ivo, after Branko translates for him by taking out all the vowels—and that's when I know Mimi sold me out.

When I lost my phone one too many times last year, she gave me the ultimatum: either stay in touch, or find other representation. I went to her dentist, and they put an RFID chip in my teeth, so she could track me down when I didn't pick up.

Not that I blame her, speaking objectively. It's the easiest fifteen percent she's ever earned off me.

Branko ignores my whining and hyperventilating until they get somewhere and stop. The rear doors fly open and someone else drags me out by the zip-ties holding my arms behind my back. The van peels out and takes off before they remove my hood, cut my zips and offer me a juice-box.

I trip on my feet and somebody else has to hold me up. "Stand on your own, you piece of shit." Finally, someone without an accent! They're sure to let me go...

Another new friend shouts in my ear, "You're here because you're worthless. Society is better off without you, and somebody very important has paid more than you've ever seen for the privilege of hunting you for sport—"

"Do you have anything besides cran-grape? This shit makes me need to pee."

"Shut up."

They stuff me into this heavy, mothball-stinking Navy pea coat and snug a watch cap down on my head. They take my loafers and belt so I can't keep my new jeans up, but some bald Vans sneakers find their way onto my feet.

Somebody clasps a mask over my face and I try not to inhale, but when I get a whiff of amyl nitrate, I'm utterly possessed and I'm running in place like that pothead on *Scooby Doo*, but I can still hear these assholes talking.

"You put too much in," the first guy says. I try to give a thumbs-up, *I'm fine*, but they're not worried about me.

"Fucking hell, it's broad daylight. We're not set up for this—"

"Bitch, please, tell someone who can do something about it. They're all butthurt because they got burned at the Globes last night. You weren't here. Came in after the after-party all coked-out like, '*We wanna kill beaners!*' and we ran out of 'em, and they won't leave, so we're down to street-meat..."

A buzzer goes off and the mask gets ripped away and I roar for more rush. The door flies open and I charge out to blasting rap-metal and they shoot me with paintballs. I panic, running over traintracks between boxcars down a chute and shooting me and the music I don't care if I die I just don't want to hear another fucking bar of Limp Bizkit...

The chute comes out under a bridge. The slick-bottom sneakers scoot down the steep, featureless concrete slope and I slide to the bottom and run pumping my fists like in the pit in an obligatory rave club scene. And then somebody starts shooting at me for real.

I always thought it was an urban legend. Actors and runaways and other locals who've been on the skids too long glibly drop it when speculating upon the fate of a vanished but unloved peer or rationalizing a dip into *scheisse*-porn or seasonal retail work, or just giving up and blowing town—"It beats the River Gig…" But hardly anyone suspects it's more than an expression, and nobody who *really* knows about the River Gig has any reason to talk about it, and if they do know it's true, no amount of coke will make them spill.

They call it the River Gig the same way they call Macbeth the Scottish Play, because there's no good that can come from naming it. But if you're so deep in debt and despair that you see no other way out, you can sign on for the River Gig, where jaded A-list sadists and industry moguls take out their frustrations by shooting you with high-power rifles as you run down the empty concrete bed of the LA River. Originally, they just picked up illegal immigrants and homeless people, but then SAG heard about it and forced them to start hiring actors.

You know that one really styling art deco bridge, it's in all the car commercials, if it's a city scene and the car is crossing an unseen river heading towards a utopian downtown skyline gleaming with the promise of bumping club tunes spun by lazy-eyed heiresses, astronomically expensive beverages and supermodel wardrobe malfunctions?

That's the starting line. The finish line is somewhere down around the 10/110 interchange, but nobody's ever reached it.

I clear a hurdle of oil barrels and shopping carts, but trip on something and go down hard. When I pop up again, sparks fly off the junk and thunder reams out my ears. I look at my feet, and realize I tripped on a dead guy.

His friend weeps and goes through his pockets, and I know he's pretty hysterical and everything, the corpse still twitching

CODY GOODFELLOW

with blood leaking out the corner of his mouth, but he ignores me when I ask him if he has any smokes.

I can smell cat turds and generic menthols on his breath. He looks dumbfounded, says something not Spanish, like Mayan or Zapotec, and weeps on his friend's chest. Then he jumps up and runs for it.

He gets maybe three steps towards the green-brown ribbon of river in the gutter of the spillway before they cut him down. He jerks and jolts in slow-motion as fans of arterial Peckinpah blood, like rubies effervescing in the rusty midmorning sun, jet out a dozen holes in his back.

What a maroon. I try to pick up his friend to use him as a human shield, but he's heavier than you.

I hear a motor roar and tires screech. I peek over the barricade. A jacked-up dunebuggy with machineguns on its rollcage peels out beside the barricade and the barrels start to spin.

I duck low and run. The guns don't track, just spit stupidly as the buggy pops into gear and starts rolling after me.

I vault over a dumpster and crawl through a length of corrugated steel pipe, scramble through a burnt-out schoolbus and out into the open and the buggy detours around the obstacle course to cut me off.

I jump off the curb and step onto the green mat of algae that spreads twenty feet out on either shore of the mighty river Porciuncula.

My foot shoots out from under me. I swim in air. I land sliding sideways on the slimy concrete—

The dunebuggy jumps the curb and hits the slime, blasting away right above my head. I'm sliding backwards watching the dunebuggy lose traction and spin spin spinning at me, spraying bullets in every direction.

I fall in the river.

It's about four and a half inches deep.

Somewhere, someone must be washing out the sluices of a meatpacking plant, the gutters of chroming vats. What I'm swimming in isn't maybe eighty percent water, but the mat of slime carries me like a hockey puck down the riverbed.

I look up just as the dunebuggy skids backwards into the river. The back wheels get mired in slime, spraying hot black mud. The driver stands and smashes his helmet against the rollcage. Cussing a blue streak I recognize from unedited video clips of every awards show after-party since '92.

Burnt at the Globes—

I wallow up on the shore of the river. "Hey, asshole! Killing me won't make those groping allegations go away!"

"Who the fuck said that?" The livid studio exec pitches his helmet in the river. "You speak *English*? God damn it, I specifically requested *Mexicans*!"

I stand up in the river. "Your lame-ass Oscar bait doesn't even rate mockery from the Razzies. When The Onion makes those flow-charts to show how crap prestige pieces get assembled, it's not a how-to guide, dude…"

The exec growls like a dog facing the guy with the neutering knife. "I'm gonna fuckin' kill you—"

"Like you killed the opening of that Tarantino movie? You couldn't open a child-proof cap without ten uncredited rewrites and a pile of Chinese hedge fund money. You fat eunuch, you couldn't manage a campaign for an Oscar Mayer hot dog."

Howling like a wounded wolf, the exec climbs out of the dunebuggy brandishing an assault rifle and falls on his ass. The gun goes off and he screams louder.

Somebody shoots me in the back.

I jerk with agony and topple back into the river. Floating facedown, blinded by a swirl of crimson, I hear shouting.

"*Motherfucker*! That was *my* kill! What are you even doing out here? We have the whole zone reserved—"

"You should've kept him in your zone, then. You're in *my* territory now, bubby."

"You cocksucker— "

They open fire on each other as I float away. They're yelling and shooting and then they yell even louder when they realize they're both shooting blanks.

I crawl up on a sandbar somewhere around City of Industry and shuck off the squib-laced overcoat among the cattails. I stagger up the temporary beach, through a thicket of wild cucumber and bamboo to a little shady grove where a dozen or so of my fellow gladiators loll and recline in the sand beside a mound, not unlike the shell-mounds that are the sole lasting evidence of many Californian coastal Indians, who dwelt in such peace that they never had a word for war or pants, only this mound is made of empty cans of spraypaint, varnish, dust removal spray and other industrial recreational pharmaceuticals. I sit down beside a sad-eyed man huffing the dregs of a can of brake degreaser, and ask him for a hit.

He shakes his head, eyes rolled back to show blank, pale yellow orbs. "This is union craft service, man. You can't get none of this unless you got a card…"

I ask who I need to see to get a voucher, but he's unconscious, so I pry open his spasming hand and suck up the last degreaser hit in the bag.

Tell me I'm not living my life right.

EIGHTEEN

[CUES: Meridian Arts Ensemble, "Caballito Nicoyano"; Mexican Institute Of Sound, "Carnaval"]

I HEAR THEY'RE REMAKING DEATH WISH WITH Bruce Willis, because white people don't buy enough guns. If the object is to sell more movie tickets and/or guns, they should do this instead.

EL TECNICO
[NOTE: This pitch could easily be reworked as a gritty modern reboot for the Zorro franchise; call me, Sony!]
So this LAPD tactical unit kicks in the kitchen door of a shitty two-bedroom bungalow in Montebello on an anonymous tip, to take down a bunch of wetbacks. They come in without knocking or identifying themselves. The first two fed thugs through the door catch a faceful of high-velocity rock salt.
Someone calls out, *Shots fired, Officer down!* The whole team goes apeshit, firing into both bedrooms. Eight guys with H&K MP5's and six more with semiautomatic shotguns and 9mm automatics unload on the house for seventy-five seconds, before the ranking agent cools them out. The whole back half of the bungalow sags on splintered joists. Somewhere under the floor, they can hear someone surrendering in broken English, and a baby crying.
They drag a little owlish Mexican guy and his wife and two

daughters—all miraculously unharmed, praise Cristo—out from under the house, and in the excitement, adrenalin running high and concern for their brother officers making everybody a little emotional, and the man may or may not stumble into a doorframe several times, giving himself a concussion and two fractured ribs. The agents search the ruins and find a single pump shotgun loaded with more rock salt, a bunch of cheap do-it-yourself electronic shit and a taco shop bag containing $9235 in cash.

They're still arguing about whether or not to stomp the sonofabitch for shooting at them, when they get two pieces of interesting news. One, the agency just settled out of court for something north of five million dollars for a raid on an innocent white middle-class family in Van Nuys.

And Two, the tac unit is in the wrong house.

Imagine their chagrin as the team's resident hedge-lawyer points out that they never identified themselves or knocked, and in this neighborhood, one could make a case that such violent entry at this ungodly hour could naturally be misinterpreted as yet another burglary. Still, there is the matter of the unpermitted shotgun and the cash. And Oswaldo Munoz isn't some white middle-class solid citizen, he's an illegal. He's nobody.

His wife doesn't expect her husband to come back alive, and when he's released without charges, she begs him to just forget about it and move on.

But Oswaldo demands a hearing. Before a judge, he tries to explain his plans for the money, his reasons for opening fire on the police. He has no criminal connections, no suspicious associates. He only wants his money back, and for the government to pay for his house. He's just a guy who was born in Oaxaca and works in a car stereo place installing alarms, but for years, he's dreamed and saved up to get an ice cream truck. Not one of those shitty carts with the bell and the ices and maybe mangos, but a real truck that plays music and everything.

The judge dismisses the case. The cashier gives him a baffling form to claim his money, but he'll need to hire a lawyer to get a penny from them, as the amount claimed ($9235) vastly differs from the amount the police reported and turned in ($235).

Friends and family tell him to leave well enough alone, move somewhere else and start over. He keeps calling the INS office and hounding the federal building about acquiring citizenship, until "gang members" in brown-face mug him and break his arm in broad daylight on Wilshire Boulevard.

He loses his job. His wife and kids get deported. He lives in his car until they find it and impound it along with the rest of his possessions.

LA eats bigger fish than Oswaldo every day and leaves not a trace. He's not a secret commando or a former sicario from the cartels who retired to the bucolic squalor of East LA like some latterday Cinncinatus. Whether he gives up and goes back to Mexico or starts over under a new name, nobody cares and nobody remembers and certainly nobody connects him with the incident that strikes terror into the hearts of the LAPD.

Fast-forward eight months. An LAPD officer pulls over a Hispanic motorist and orders him out of the car. The truck has a burnt-out taillight, but the cop is having a shit night and couldn't get it up with a USC freshman coed he caught trying to score coke for sorority rush week. So he pulls the guy out of his truck and proceeds to go full piñata on his ass, when a red laser pointer light paints his face. He looks around and sees a guy in a luchador mask aiming a rifle at him on a nearby rooftop, just before he gets shot in the face.

He screams for backup, claiming he's been shot, but when the cops, the ambulance and the obligatory media stringer van show up, they find he's been hit in the face with several paintballs, only they've got that same indelible dye they hide in the cash when you try to rob a bank. Now and forever, he'll have to wear a whole paintcan of makeup to hide looking like the clown he'll forever see in the mirror.

And without ever killing anybody, Oswaldo declares war on the government.

Cops and ICE agents respond to tips on illegal aliens and

CODY GOODFELLOW

reports of armed men on rooftops, only to find themselves ambushed and marked with red dye. When ICE's top cop announces a manhunt for the Mexican Marauder, as the press dubs him, every car alarm for a two-mile radius goes off, and the microphone at the press conference explodes with red and green dye, painting a Mexican flag on the pasty white fed's face.

The Latino community embraces Munoz as a brown Robin Hood. They call him el Tecnico, after the trope of the heroic luchador wrestler, and knockoffs of his mask sell out everywhere and throng the streets, triggering constant false alarm calls.

A full-fledged crackdown ensues, but while they roust and deport thousands, ICE just can't seem to get their hands on the right Mexican. Millions of them want only to work their asses off to support their families, but they all slink around guiltily because of their immigration status, and the more the feds bust, beat and seize, somehow they come off looking like the real terrorists... until a brilliant Latina agent brainwashed into mistaking her ambition for patriotism combs through ICE's old raids and identifies Oswaldo Munoz as the real perpetrator.

ICE lays out a brilliant trap for Munoz by placing ads in Spanish-only newspapers for a FREE giveaway of recently impounded ice cream trucks. Munoz knows it's a trap, but he shows up anyway, determined to give the government one last chance to make good on what they took from him.

The ICE agents lock the doors and inform the hundred-odd prospective ice cream truck owners that they're under arrest for terrorism, pending fingerprinting.

A man puts on a Tecnico mask and walks to the exit. An overeager agent shoots the man when he refuses to stop. As one, the group of men put on masks and proclaim, "Yo soy el tecnico," and refuse to be fingerprinted. As the men are arrested and beaten, it's discovered that none of them has fingerprints at all.

Meanwhile, the news begins to roll in from across the Southland. It's bad.

A general strike has been called by the Mexican immigrant

community. Farming, meatpacking, catering, trucking, construction, garment, toy and electronics manufacturing industries grind to a halt. Phone calls to all local, state and federal government agencies yield only more confusion for anyone who won't "Marque Ocho para Español," because the automated operators speak only Spanish.

Chaos percolates upwards as millions miss work when their housekeepers and nannies fail to show up. Riots break out in Beverly Hills and Century City as wealthy white patrons are forced to try to make their own breakfasts. Faced with the biggest labor crisis in its history, the economy grinds to a halt, and the business lobby orders government to settle. But having denigrated them and refused to take them seriously as a demographic group for decades, the government can't find a credible representative with whom to negotiate. Everyone they reach out to says the same thing: *Talk to el tecnico.*

With the state teetering on the brink of martial law and Mexico offering to send aid and peacekeeping troops, the brilliant but regretful Latina ICE agent leaves the bedlam of her office to stand on the sweltering street as uncollected trash blows by and white people in late stages of scurvy search in vain for someone selling oranges, when she hears the soothing chimes of an ice cream truck playing Malaguena Salerosa.

She flags down the truck and asks the owlish little Mexican man inside for a snow-cone. When he gives it to her—cherry, coconut and lime, with a little brown sugar eagle on top—she sticks her gun in his face and orders *el tecnico* to surrender and call off the strike.

The snow-cone explodes in her face, dyeing her permanently with the colors of the flag she abandoned, and for what?

El tecnico drives off into the sunset, as the ice cream chimes of La Malaguena are taken up by a full orchestra.

But sure, remake *Death Wish* with Bruce Willis instead. That'll be fun, too.

CODY GOODFELLOW

NINETEEN

[CUES: Major Lazer, "Get Free"; Philip Glass, "Osamu's Theme: Kyoko's House"; Tangerine Dream, "Betrayal (Sorcerer Theme)"]

HITCHHIKING IS HARD ENOUGH WHEN YOU didn't literally just crawl out of the sewer. I climb out of a storm drain, tear my pants on the ragged chainlink fence and before I can even stick my thumb out, there's a cop car.

Panic. I try to jump back over the fence. My pants rip up the inseam and I'm dangling sideways, trying to twist away from the rusty spikes gouging my inner thigh, headed with evil intent towards my crotch.

Even I know that running away from the police is a capital offense. They're only supposed to shoot you to defend their own lives, but forcing a middle-aged rageaholic in tactical body armor to run more than a city block is potentially life-threatening.

"Hey fella, you're gonna hurt yourself!"

Oh thank God, a witness, I think, but the warm, concerned voice is coming from the cop. Big white guy with a pornstache and silver at his temples; steely, hooded eyes and his hands up like he's approaching a scared mule deer caught in an electric fence.

For all I know, he's been called to return me to the River Gig. In a movie, he's either one of them, or his brains will get blown in my face the moment I begin to feel safe. The cops who come on nice and friendly are the worst, like a cat playing with its food.

"Let me help you, son."

"I'm not doing anything wrong…"

"Beg pardon, young man, but if you're trying to run back into the sewer, then it's safe to say you're probably doing something wrong. Why not try something different, and let somebody help you?"

What the fuck? In the calculus of cop talk, this means the fucking sadist is going to sodomize me with my own dislocated arm the moment I give in.

I kick him in the face. He lifts me off the fence and stands me up and steps back with his filth-encrusted hands up. Rubbing mud off his jaw, he takes a deep breath and says, "Listen, I understand you're having a bad day. If you've got somewhere to go and clean yourself up, then you're welcome to. But I was just about to go to lunch, and I'd be happy to drop you off anywhere you need to go…"

I take another step back, wondering what kind of evil John Wayne Gacy motherfucker plays twisted games with his prey like this. Something is seriously wrong here, and it's not just the cop. But I'm so very fucking tired of running. "I don't want to ride in the back…"

"That's fine, you can ride up front with me. You can even work the radio, if you like."

I'm *dead*.

So fucking *dead*.

I can't look at the cop. When I look, he'll have clown makeup on and he'll lean in and bite my face off and the last thing I feel will be rancid greasepaint smeared into the raw exposed muscles of my screaming skull.

He thumps me in the chest with something.

"Go ahead and put these on."

"No way. What the…?"

"They're my street clothes." I go behind the open passenger door and drop my pants, step into a baggy pair of sweats. A yard of fabric billows around each ankle and I have to contrive a knot in the waistband, but the shirt hangs almost to my knees to cover it. At least they're not encrusted with industrial sewage, so I put them on under duress, holding my nose against the gross fabric softener perfume clinging to the I DONATED BLOOD T-shirt.

In the car. Riding in the front seat. He lets me work the radio. I can't get LA on this thing. Traffic accidents, a couple dogs running around loose in the Pershing Square farmer's market, but where are the robberies, the road rage incidents, the "black or Hispanic" suspect description that fit anyone browner than you, the *No Humans Involved* shootings south of the 10?

Hog the mic. Sure he's taking me to a Dogpile Call, he'll phone it in any minute. Cops get wound up and start popping off on duty, knocking heads at home, the department hates to admit it, but stats don't lie. Only one thing seems to take the edge off: tuning up with extreme prejudice on a helpless misdemeanor offender, preferably a young adult of no observable means, if nobody of color is handy. When you come across ten squad cars on a corner and a knot of cops making like the Demon Drummers of Kodo on a single, prone black or Hispanic punching bag, don't take a picture, just keep walking. Group therapy is like sleepwalking; dangerous to interrupt.

"Are you OK?" The cop offers me a paper carton of water and a slightly bruised Granny Smith apple bigger than my fist, then takes it back. "What am I thinking, these apples are heck on an empty stomach."

I look out the window, but I can't find LA. South of downtown and east of Alameda, the gray blocks are filled with a utopian combo of businesses no sane resident wants anywhere near them, and a lot of indifferently housed and homeless people who nobody listens to.

This LA looks like an electric car commercial. No tents or tarp lean-tos in every crack. No dingy factories. The people on the street don't look rich, but they're not starving or fat, they flit by on schools of bicycles without getting run over. Then I notice something else.

Green.

Except for weeds and the occasional leafless landscaping trees staked out on the sidewalk like petrified prisoners of war, nothing grows downtown. But every block flashes a blur of green. Pocket parks, jogging trails. The trees on every corner are dripping tangerines and apples, and nobody gets a ticket or a truncheon to the kidneys for picking and eating them as they pass. I watch some fucker toss orange peels at a trashcan, then turn and blow off the crossing light to pick up the bits that ended up on the sidewalk.

We pass the brown brutalist tower of the county jail, but it's not there and instead, a soccer field. Tatted up guys in long white shirts and baggy jeans play with a couple men and women in suits and ties, a couple black guys and another cop. Everybody smiling and hustling downfield after a goalie's free throw, just a random cross-section of downtown Los Angeles enjoying a pickup game on a late lunch hour in blithe denial of racial, class and social barriers as rigid as any in Christendom.

I get it now.

This isn't my LA.

This isn't even Earth.

These aren't humans.

I want to find the right way to ask how long ago Canada took over, but this isn't even like the LA the biblebangers ruined. Union Station is still there, thank God, but did they film *Blade Runner*, *Bugsy*, *Pearl Harbor*, *Silver Streak*, *Under The Rainbow*, *Drag Me To Hell* and *Trancers II: The Return Of Jack Deth* here? Does the *Trancers* franchise even exist in this fucked-up parallel universe?

We go into a Korean taco-donut place and I look at the menu and there's no pastrami burritos, no carne asada, no meat whatsoever, and the cop and the Korean guy both look at me like I'm not speaking any human language when I ask. So I order a huge jelly donut and some coffee and sit down and the "jelly" is some kind of freshly cut pineapple-apricot business that gives me diabetes.

CODY GOODFELLOW

He tells me he didn't want to hassle me, but if I need a few bucks for a proper meal, he'd be happy to lend it to me. "Just pay it forward to the next person you see who needs it."

"Nah, I'm good. I just gotta get back up to Hollywood to see my agent and pick up a residual check…" He's staring at me. "Commercial gig. European. Not surprised you haven't seen it, but over there, man… I'm like… huge."

The cop just nods and smiles sadly. "So… having a bad day?"

"Yeah, kinda… I'm just trying to catch up with this girl…"

"Ohhhhh, I got you." He nods slyly, but not leering. "And, uh… when you find her…"

"She needs my help. Really. I was minding my own business, and then she came up on me, and everything since then's been a total shitshow, but I really think—"

"That if you can help her, it'll make some sort of sea change in your own life, which has been out of control for as long as you can remember. Right?"

I shrug.

"And you're thinking that if you save someone else, you'll redeem yourself in the eyes of a world that has rejected you, and you'll find the courage to be who you really are, instead of always hiding behind masks. Am I getting warmer?"

Shrug harder. Just kill me, already, Maniac Cop.

"Sure, I understand that, as far as it goes. But what about *after*? Assuming you reclaim your life. What's your plan?"

Shrug with extreme prejudice. "I… want to go into—I mean, totally *crush* TV, and, you know, movies." And for the first time ever, it lays like rancid cat food on my tongue. For the first time ever, just saying it like that, it sounds kind of stupid. "It's all I ever wanted."

He blinks. "Why?"

"What do you mean, *why?*"

"I mean, why do you want to be on TV? It just doesn't seem like it'd be very… satisfying…"

"What the fuck? Of course it'd be satisfying, like… to be

rich and famous..."

The cop tries very hard to nod and smile. "That's a good idea, if it really makes you happy... but... I mean it's no substitute for... Well, let's not even get into that. Do you even have a teaching credential?"

"*What*?"

"Well... I mean, they don't have just *anyone* on TV... No offense... People like to learn something when they tune in, but sometimes, if you have a special talent or skill, they'll hire you to sing or dance. I mean, even bus drivers get more chances to actually help people..."

"Wrong. It's like that old saying, Give a man fish, and he'll eat the fish, but teach him to fish, and he'll feed himself."

"That's very wise," says the cop.

"But show him a movie about fishing, and he'll buy your fish, and your branded ancillary merchandise."

"I don't follow."

"You're a cop, and you probably help a few people sometimes, and that's cool. And I could become a cop and help people too, maybe, but people will still think I'm an asshole, because everybody hates cops."

He looks genuinely wounded. "I don't think that's true—"

"No, trust me, they do. But if I act like the best cop ever in a movie, a latterday knight errant fighting for justice in a crooked, dangerous world, then people will treat cops like human beings."

"Wait... so you want to *pretend* to be a cop on the television? Who the heck would want to watch that?"

"I mean, I've got a lot more range, but..."

He looks at me like I want to be on exhibit in the zoo. "I don't know where you get your ideas from, friend, but it sounds pretty screwed up. These TV people of yours pay you to pretend to be other things, and you make a living at it?"

"Yeah. We're the most beloved and respected humans on the planet."

"That's just... that'd be like paying people good money to play hide and seek, or basketball..." He pokes at his food, genuinely troubled. "But if you feel like it's what you're here to do, by gosh, you should go try out for it. I mean, if you're serious about it, but…"

"It's not that easy."

"Sure it is. I mean, it doesn't pay very well… A lot of TV presenters are retired doctors and teachers… but if you ask me, some of those nature documentaries they put out in the summertime are getting too flashy for their own good…"

He clears his throat, a low, gurgling forever noise, and coughs into a handkerchief, drops it on the table. He leans in close. "I'm thinking I just figured out what's going on here."

I nearly throw up. He had his windows down in the car, so I didn't realize at first what was wrong.

"I'm sorry," he says. "It's just… your breath. He says, "You're *uncultured*."

My breath?

What about *his* breath?

It's like an overloaded porta-shitter at a chili cook-off. Not hungry breath or halitosis, or thrush, or tooth decay. It's EXACTLY the smell of human feces, of a freshly pinched-off pie, unadulterated by water or air fresheners.

Dookie-breath.

This is my least favorite LA.

He looks at me kind of funny, then offers me a breath mint.

I put my hand over my mouth and check my breath. It smells like that dastardly fruit compote and a pretty decent cup of coffee. I accept the "mint" from him. It practically sizzles with the same septic miasma oozing from his sad smile. I palm it, pocket it and surreptitiously put a Listerine lozenge on my tongue instead. "What do you mean? I mean, what you said before—about being 'uncultured'? I read a book all the time."

He shrugs, fingering the radio on his belt. I notice then, I don't know why I didn't notice before. The cop doesn't have a gun. Or cuffs. "You know what I mean… Your tongue isn't coated. Your breath, it's… *dead*. No offense… but don't worry. The mint I gave you should fix the problem. Balance your oral bacteria."

"Oh, that. Sure, I can feel it working. It's, uh… Why're you looking at me like that?"

The cop ruefully shakes his head and says, *"Forgive me."* He lunges across the table. He knocks me out of my chair, pins me to the floor and plants his reeking mouth on mine.

I fucking *knew* it. Cops never just *give away* donuts…

His tongue thrusts into my mouth and scrapes itself off on my teeth, painting my recoiling tongue with sticky, fecal crud. I try to kick out, to push him away, but all I succeed in doing is spitting the Listerine lozenge into his mouth.

He recoils and scoots all the way to the wall, knocking over chairs and clutching his throat as yellow-brown bile and foam sprays from his mouth and nostrils. The Korean cashier comes around the counter with his phone at his ear, talking animatedly while trying to calm me down.

I stand and look around. The foam keeps spewing out of the cop's mouth. I pick up the handkerchief and wrap it around his car keys and run for the door.

I come outside into blazing sunlight needles in my eyes so I walk right into the punch.

She hits me just above my drooping waistband. I fold over the fist and trip off the curb. Some other hands catch me by the collar of my shirt and a third pair of hands takes my ankles, and they all carry me across the lot to the police car and toss me in the back.

My captors are the donut cook, a young black guy in a parking valet's uniform and a small Vietnamese manicurist. The lady drives the cop car out of the lot and into the street. The valet sits next to me and the cook sits up front, holding the shotgun. None of them look like there's anything weird about them driving a cop car. Nothing weird about it at all, until their fecal mildew breath begins to pervade the car.

"Crack a window, for the love of God!"

"You're the only one around here who stinks," the valet says.

If we could perceive our own foulness, would we not be more forgiving of others? I do still smell pretty strongly of the sewer. "Where're you taking me?"

"Where do you belong?"

"I'm from another LA, where people with minty fresh breath lie to each other all the time... I won't give out any more Listerine, I promise. I just want to go back..."

"How can you do that?"

"Just let me concentrate..." It's not happening.

"What are you trying to do?" the driver asks.

"We should just kill him," the cook says. "He can't stay."

"I don't *want* to stay!"

"What are you trying to do?" the valet asks.

"Stop breathing on me! I'm trying to get into character..."

"What's he doing?" the manicurist asks.

"It's called *acting.*"

"Acting like what?"

"Like I'm not *here*, damn it!" I sit up and bang my head against the bars in frustration. "Would you please crack a window?"

And that's when I realize the car is empty, except for me. And it's still moving.

TWENTY

THIS WOULD WORK AS A MOTION PICTURE franchise or a TV series for a forward-thinking pay-cable outlet.

We open on Sam Reed, a young widow forced to move to the city to find work when the bank takes the family farm. With his young son and daughter in tow, Sam ends up in a lousy, dangerous part of town and has to struggle and bribe and beg just to land a job working in the sewer.

Up to his knees in putrid rivers of shit morning, noon and night, Sam toils thanklessly to keep the city's principal export product flowing, until the day when all the pipes freeze up, and then begin to flow *backwards*, flooding every home, business, movie studio, government office, port-a-potty and honey wagon in Los Angeles with a deadly torrent of noxious solid waste... but the real horror is just beginning.

Because somewhere in the sewer, a revolution has broken out. The sea of shit beneath our feet has come to life. It has awakened and risen to wage bloody warfare on the thoughtless humans who spawned and then rejected it.

Trapped in Ground Zero of the shitpocalypse, Sam and an ethnically and genderically diverse ensemble of quirky, crotchety and sassy urban characters fights their way out of the sewers and across the blasted city to be reunited with his children, but what kind of world has he saved them for?

Corpses everywhere lie burst open in the street, where impacted fecal matter erupted out of them like horrible brown butterflies. Each of Sam's newfound friends in turn sacrifices himself at a critical point to help Sam and his kids escape the city, but when they finally encounter a group of his old country friends who have banded together into a militia to protect themselves from roving bands of humans as well as hordes of shit-people, they learn that the next phase of the invasion has begun, and hope is all but lost.

In the sequel/second season, following the *Alien/Aliens* model, we pivot from high-concept survival horror to a wider action/war dialectic. The Shitosphere has solidified its hideous gains, and organized, even evolved a crude parody of self-awareness.

Everywhere men used to walk, it shambles on two legs and seems to speak and think and act in a monstrous imitation of humanity. As stumbling, stinking nightsoil men swarm the empty boulevards, restaurants, bars, offices and studios and start taking all the jobs, mountainous colonies of live sewage from the treatment plants and septic tanks expand to cover whole neighborhoods, rendering them uninhabitable to humanity. Bubbling, reeking bedpans of filth take to the airwaves to proclaim that they will no longer tolerate such degrading epithets as "shit," "poop" or "ca-ca."

Henceforth, Feco-Americans will be entitled to the same rights, privileges and entitlements as all other American citizens. They were born here, they're not going anywhere, and they outnumber us hundreds of millions to one, and every high-fiber meal the doomed humans consume only adds to the invaders' numbers.

Sam and his militia friends have only just scraped off their shoes when they find a whole new peril waiting to be stepped in. The United Nations has quarantined North America, and ordered the U.S. government to recognize walking piles of shit as citizens and to submit to be married to and interbred with their own feces in order to gradually absorb the problem.

Sam sets out with his comrades to strike a critical blow against the Feco-American occupiers, blasting the Hoover Dam to flood Las Vegas and wash away the legions of shitheads filling the casinos.

Sam brings his family to the last compound of unconquered humanity in all North America, in the Colorado Rockies. A great victory has been won, but the endgame looms before them as the combined solid waste of the most overfed nation on Earth prepares to come crashing down on their heads.

Naturally, my trenchant social commentary went right over their heads. Even if I offered a bonus reacharound, I could never get any serious producers to stick around long enough to read the whole trilogy. "That was so racist, I can't even come in your mouth," was probably the nicest thing anyone had to say about THE WALKING TURDS project.

But the very next fall season, AMC rolls out THE WALKING DEAD, and Universal puts these walking clumps of baby-shit in *Despicable Me* and then gives them their own franchise.

Do I have to draw you a flow-chart?

TWENTY-ONE

[CUES: Midge Ure, "The Chieftain"; Max Romeo & The Upsetters, "I Chase The Devil"]

I'M ROLLING DOWN THE GREEN TILED TUNNEL from *Blade Runner, Repo Man* and *Heat* and the police car jumps the curb and stalls out nosed against the wall. I try the doors—no handles—and kick the windows—bullet-proof—and make faces at passing motorists, but nobody slows down or stops. I try to take comfort in their indifference. They may not care if I die, but their breath is probably no worse than it ought to be.

Somebody comes over and gets behind the wheel. "Shit, I didn't think we were gonna find a ride." He turns the key in the ignition and guns it, backs up off the curb so someone else can climb in the passenger seat.

I sit up. Naturally, it's more cops. Except…

The guy behind the wheel is wearing an old Parker-era black polyester uniform with the long-sleeved tunic and a peaked cap, and the passenger is a Keystone Kop in a moth-eaten midnight-blue woolen tunic with a big star and a row of silver buttons, and a high, domed helmet with another big star on it.

When you're driving a stolen police car, it's important to look like you know what you're doing. Drive slow and steady. Don't turn on the siren or otherwise call attention to yourself by driving up the wrong side of the road in post-lunch traffic. All of which these assholes are doing.

I'm closing my eyes and willing myself out of the car, and when that fails, I work on our backstory.

We're delivering a prop car to a location shoot. Our papers are in transit, the printer jammed, but if the diligent officer wants to call Paramount's bitchy Transport Manager and sit on hold for fifteen minutes before finding out his shift captain is trying to get hold of him with a 1ˢᵗ AD from the shoot chewing his other ear off, that's *his* fucking business…

Life doesn't just imitate art here, it bends over backward for it.

Another speeding cop car comes up alongside us, and the guys inside are wearing ninja and samurai outfits and Viking helmets with horns shredding the headliners and they pass the Keystone Kop a joint as we blast through every red light going to the 101. We scream up the offramp and blaze the carpool lane going north on the southbound, and I pump my fist and cheer gang graffiti and sheriff's helicopters and smog and billboards for the latest *Saw* sequel. The Kop's breath smells like vinegar and cough syrup. He sticks the joint through the bars so I can hit it.

We join a gigantic movie motorcade up the 101 to Gower and turn north, into the hills, following the earwax yellow placards with the shoot's coded title and arrows pointing north. Cruisers, SWAT vans, paddy wagons, black mariahs, motorcycles, schoolbuses, firetrucks, hovercraft, half-tracks, Roman chariots, cowboys and Indians on horseback and a platoon of elephants with archers riding on howdahs to shoot out the tires of anyone who gets in our way.

If I had any doubt about the city outside, the flocks of teen runaways, tubby tourists and street freaks streaming down Hollywood reassure me that I'm home. These people might have a million different problems, but bacterial infections that turn them into contented, productive citizens isn't one of them.

These guys are my best friends until we get to the talent parking lot. They ask if I have a SAG/AFTRA card, and when I admit I don't, they dump me on the corner of Franklin and Bronson. A Peterbilt truck towing a trailer with three tiers of cop cars bulls through the tourist traffic, and my erstwhile friends follow it.

All the traffic down here is cop cars. Real ones. And I realize I look quite a bit like my composite sketch, now.

I climb into the hills on foot. Pass the NO HOLLYWOOD SIGN ACCESS signs that edify and deter absolutely no one, the gauntlet of labyrinthine slaloms and non-Euclidean Moebius strip intersections and security patrols in golfcarts with serious mission-creep confusion about their spheres of authority; up past the ceiling of smog to the rarified cul-de-sac warrens of the truly great.

Goons in valet uniforms push a hatchback with Nebraska plates over the curb and down into a blind box canyon to make room for a phlegm-yellow Lamborghini Montepulciano. Two more bitch-slap a prominent reality TV editor with his own newspaper as he protests their parking Shaq's monster truck and an Escalade in his driveway. They grab their crotches and flip Hitler salutes my way when I ask who they're working for.

Every failure in LA comes away with pretty much the same story. *I sucked, nobody cared, The End.* The scariest ones are the success stories.

Up on the street I'm looking for, there's plenty of parking. Two cars are discreetly spaced a few houses from the house I'm looking for, just on the edge of the curving street that affords them a clear view of the front of the house. A plainclothes police detective empties a thermos of piss into the gutter; the studio dick on the other side dumps a bucket of cigarette butts into the neighbor's award-winning roses.

The narrow, unassuming facade midway between them is the front of a nine-bedroom hillside monstrosity that spills down into the canyon and gorges itself on the backyards of four adjacent properties to make a massive arcadian sanctuary rife with screeching peacocks. Its owner is under strict covert house arrest with a tracking bracelet and subject to surprise drug and alcohol tests by either the state or the studio. And I'm not allowed to use their name, which should tell you something, given how indiscreet I've been up to now, but there's some things even I know not to fuck with. This personage pretty much only gets to leave the house to shoot or promote films and accept awards, and to sue anyone who breathes a negative rumor.

Not even the national media outlets can score a sit-down interview with this person right now, but I am not going to visit this person, who is officially, as anyone who reads *Variety* knows, in the middle of a thirteen-week shoot in Austria, Turkey and the Maldives, but who is really, as anyone with the inside track knows, currently drying out after blowing off a press tour while stand-ins, stuntmen and rendered CG captures from previous films do all the heavy lifting.

When private security comes rushing over and pins me down on the driveway so my baggy sweats sop up layers of scorched motor oil and cat litter, I tell them who I'm here to see, and they vaporize after a cursory cavity search.

When I get inside, Propaganda's "Sorry For Laughing" blasts from speakers set into ceiling and floor. A battle-scarred Big Trak passes by with a can of Like Cola in its freight bed, so I follow it through the atrium and down a murky, mildewy hall to Kevin's office. The Big Trak muffs the last turn and grinds its gears butting against the wall inches short of the doorway. Kevin wouldn't have fucked up the programming, so the house must be growing.

So there's this normal, healthy guy, and like millions of normal, healthy American middle-class white guys, Kevin lives in his mom's basement. Such a decent kid, even when he's alone in his house, he pees against the side of the bowl so no one hears the sound of his urine hitting water. Never could pee in public at all.

Born in 1990, his subterranean lair is a shrine to the 80's, particularly to early console videogames and obscure synthpop music. Every wall is floor-to-ceiling shelves of vinyl records and bound fanzines, videogames displayed by platform and manufacturer, and a horde of mostly functional vintage synthesizers liberated from pawnshops and thrift stores when the bottom fell out of the hardware market. Frozen in an era just before his birth and two steps short of emotional puberty, Kevin dicks around making retro pop tunes under dorky sobriquets like Vangelousy and Moroder Incorporated for bragging rights with other hardcore synth dorks on throwback gearhead message boards.

About the only current cultural phenomenon this guy keeps up on is the career of a particular film star. Kevin has always found his favorite star's films refreshing because they never have a love interest shoehorned awkwardly into the plot to satisfy some accountant's idea of a bankable date movie. In a recurring dream he had throughout his teen years, he hit the showers with his favorite film star after completing a successful daredevil mission together, and our friend was ambiguously shocked to discover that the action figures made in China of his idol were anatomically correct, for he had no more pretense of secondary sexual characteristics than any Ken or Barbie, just a blank pelvic arch with no reproductive or excretory organs whatsoever.

And then his favorite star announces that he's doing a fic-rock-biopic set in the 1980's and he'll be composing and performing the songs himself, and our introverted friend is riven by warring impulses. In the end, his need to reach out wins out over his crippling shyness, and he sends a demo of some of his choicest retro songs.

His online friends remind him major celebrities get mountains of fan mail every day, rafts of spec scripts by toe-sucking, slobbering fans hoping to conjure themselves into the celebrity's dream world. He forgets about it with a frenzy of impulse-buy South Korean bootleg Colecovision cartridges.

Until the movie comes out, and he hears his masterpiece, his most personal instrumental electro tune—"Bipolar Hi-Roller (Shamanic Depressive Club Mix)"—in a fucking training montage. Like so many ill-advised vanity vehicles, the movie is dumped in February and bombs even in China, but the unkindest cut of all is that our wallflower's name isn't listed in the credits block. He didn't expect any money for it, but some acknowledgment would've been nice. The fucking guy took credit for his song. The asshole's people won't take his calls, just simper patronizingly as he fumes and rages and schemes to take his idol to court.

At this point, any competent therapist could've pointed out how his fixation with this particular celebrity represented a profound sublimation of his own repressed sexuality, and that the delusion of entitlement was an extraordinary projection of his own sexual desire on a film star who was himself plagued by recurring rumors of closeted homosexuality.

This last would've sent up all sorts of red flags, and they probably would've advised against our friend traveling to Southern California to demand satisfaction. But nobody did.

So he flies down and hires a cab to cruise the actor's neighborhood and gets dropped off and within minutes, he's arrested and beaten senseless by Bel Air Patrol. While the LAPD would've processed him at Parker Center after having beaten him until they'd overcome their deep-seated feelings of impotence and self-loathing, the security goons deliver him to the tender mercies of the actor himself, who tips them handsomely not to notify the real police.

As it was explained to him later, since he wasn't sexually attractive to any of the subhuman groupie posse that dwell under the actor's house, if he'd just kept his mouth shut, he would've been allowed to escape; but he made such a pest of himself over his stupid song, that he got the actor all paranoid, and so our hapless protag is cast into a lightless hell of pain and humiliation.

What happens to him over the next several months, he is not willing to tell, and most likely blocked out to preserve his fragile sanity. Somewhere along the way, he develops a severe facial tic, a nasty case of herpes and all his body hair falls out and fails to grow back.

But in a reversal of fortune worthy of a bouncy John Hughes montage, this guy goes from a drooling, twitching spastic degraded worse than John Hurt at the end of *1984*, to the de facto head of household. Locked in the trash shed, he reorganizes the recycling; moved to the laundry closet, he folds everything and puts it all away without needing a map; from cooking and cleaning to making out the grocery list for the Gelson's delivery, from licking the bathroom floors clean to answering the actor's mountains of fan mail and finally making out the household budget and scheduling the actor's media appearances.

Far from being a parasite on the family tit back home, our friend was once the cornerstone of a local independent medical billing operation, for his terror of confronting other people in the flesh is only exceeded by his precise and exacting sense of detail with all inanimate objects and other people's schedules and finances.

Before the first anniversary of his disappearance, he's not only free, but an authorized user of his deranged, dissolute idol's credit cards. Now free to leave, he finds that the monster who stole his dreams is now completely dependent upon him. For the first time in his life, he feels truly appreciated by someone else. Besides, he has nowhere else to go, since his mother sold every last piece of his lovingly assembled 80's collection within a week of his leaving the basement.

The house feels like a haunted Swedish art gallery—chrome, blonde wood, white leather, firefly track-lighting and the shittiest collection of modern art and whatever framed wood is, this side of the Pompidou. All except Kevin's office.

Black steel and mirrors, obsessively recreating the billionaire's suite room from *Wolfen*, give or take a couple Nagel and Mapplethorpe prints. A beautiful double-edged gesture for someone who loves the 80's as much as he hates mirrors.

The whole place is spotless and I've never seen an animal on the premises, and yet the whole place reeks of piss. I've never found the right way to bring it up. Kevin is almost always either too frigid or too fragile for frank conversation. Only when you've walked a few thousand milligrams in another man's medicine chest, can you truly know his heart. Kevin knows mine well enough to lock up the whole west wing, and all the drugs and alcohol.

I go inside and set the dewy, thirty-year old can of Like Cola on the desk. He's been obsessed with rebuilding his old console game collection, but he's only about twenty percent there, and never has time to play. *River Raid* runs on autopilot on a screen above his head, a node of eight-bit serenity amid gnashing walls of TMZ clips and Twitter feeds and old MTV videos and cartoons.

Propaganda fades out. The Stranglers' "All Roads Lead To Rome" fades in. "Nice Big Trak, Kev. It's the original '79 version?"

He doesn't dignify the question with a response. "I'm sorry, but we both know that's ridiculous," he finally says, but not to me. "He never gets out of bed for less than ten K."

"Programming must be drifting on it... Missed the last turn. Left a nasty scuff on the baseboard..."

He shrugs, eyes flitting from one to another of four monitors above his desk as he makes notes on the chittering canary noises in his ear. The Stranglers fade out. His headset keens with the caller's irate reply. Pet Shop Boys' "Opportunities" comes on. Don't you fucking hate on-the-nose music cues?

"That's funny, Avi. Tell you what. You look under some cushions and call me back when you can scrape up ten grand, and we'll come down there, and who knows, maybe he *will* cure your skin cancer. Heal the maimed and the halt and the blind. No, don't think about it, you melanoma-raddled putz. His rate goes up next week, and you're hardly the only tanning place in West Hollywood."

Kevin hangs up and whips off the headset, rips it apart and drops it in the wastebasket between his knees. The smell of vomit in it is almost stronger than the mysterious pee smell.

He has to go through this every time his boss needs a haircut or a reflexology alignment or a dental cleaning. Not only won't he pay, but they're supposed to pay his public appearance fee, just to get him in the door. If he has to go out like a regular nobody, a makeup artist comes over to do his "disguise," which takes two hours, and most won't come over for any amount of money. Thus, Kevin has had to get trained, if not officially licensed, as a beautician, manicurist, chiropractor, holistic healer and exterminator.

"Pretty big party going on somewhere nearby," I say. "You know who's throwing it?"

Artfully, he shakes his body without lifting his head off the keyboard. With his tongue, he types FUKOFF.

"I need a favor."

He executes an artful interpretive dance composed entirely of shrugs.

"I need help finding a girl. I think the Psylosophists have her."

He stops.

Takes out a fresh headset.

Takes a drink of Like Cola.

Reaches for the remote and fades the music down just as the nasal chorus comes whining in. "Why would we know anything about that?"

I start to say, "But—"

"Because we don't."

"But," I hasten to cut in—

"It's well-documented that we're not involved in any religious activity, though we still attend holiday services at Christmas and Easter with our family in the church where we were christened, in Idaho Falls, Arizona. Our spirituality is a deeply personal matter, between us and…"

The most beautiful naked woman I've ever seen in the flesh saunters into the room, holding a feather duster.

Kevin pokes me in the neck, rudely cutting off my airflow and bloodflow in one open-handed stroke. *"Don't look at her, asshole,"* he says in an acidic whisper.

She goes over to the far corner of the room, lazily dabbing at a wall unit lined with Activision 2600 cartridges, squats in the corner with her back to us, disappears behind the display of *Inhumanoids* toys.

I start to ask. Kevin cocks his arm to punch me and shakes his head. "She charges double if you give her a hard time," he whispers.

"What, exactly, constitutes a 'hard time'?" I try to emulate his legendary shrug. I impress myself. "Come on, man. It's just me. I'm not looking for an exclusive. I just need a line on where—"

"We know *nothing* about it."

I grab him by the epaulets on his Members Only jacket and whip him around to face me. "Everybody knows your boy is—"

"—fucking bullshit rumors—"

"—the nuttiest nut in the fucking fruitcake."

"Get out."

A devastating retort dies a horrible, flaming death in my throat. With a ladylike grunt, the gorgeous naked woman finishes urinating on the carpet. Stands up and struts by, picking up Kevin's unfinished Like and draining it, dropping the empty can on the floor beside the wastebasket on her way out.

I point to the fresh cigarette burn on the back of his hand. "That's pretty bad, dude. Is your boss still burning you?"

"I… He… he's going through a lot, right now."

"Yeah, he's pretty busy. He phones you from Bangkok, or wherever he really is, to tell you where, and for how long? Does that really do it for him, still? I would think he could line up some ladyboy loser here in town, that he could pick up through Grindr or something… Kev, are you okay, you look all flushed and *jealous*…"

It's wonderful when someone comes out to LA and finds out who they really are, if they can face it. It's not so easy to find out you *belong* in somebody else's closet.

"I don't expect you to understand. He's here…"

"Where?"

"I'm not going to parade him out for you…"

"Because you can't, because he blew town."

"That's not…"

I kick his ankle. "Why're you wearing his tracking bracelet?"

Kevin crosses his legs. "You'll never understand."

"Oh, but I *do*, man. There's no more toxic substance to the human heart than unrequited love."

"See? You don't get it at all." He notices me surfing his shoulder, blanks all the screens and turns around in his chair. Predictable as shark attacks on sweeps week. Good thing I only showed interest once I'd finished reading.

Fingers in so many pies… His Master buys concept and expressionist and process art projects from struggling artists and releases them as his own, to give him an edgy cachet without distracting from his commitment to doing two or more lucrative slabs of multiplex stupography every year. This wildly expensive vanity project forces him to diversify his portfolio into other questionable high risk ventures…

A variation on the nasal intubation system used for force-feeding hunger-strikers and coma patients recast in bright plastic for stubborn, finicky kids. A low-budget airline that sedates its passengers and hangs them in pouches like sides of beef, three hundred and fifty to a plane. And some *really* stupid ideas…

"He's feeling hemmed in by acting, isn't he? Looking to branch out, do some good in the real world…"

"If you're looking for work," he says, digging around in the thicket of post-its on the desk and crawling up the walls like scabrous yellow ivy, "I can get you background work on the new Duchovny show…"

"I've been in the background my entire fucking life, man. *I* want to do some good in the real world. I want to know what it feels like actually help someone—not one of us… A *real* person."

"It feels like this," he says, rolling up his sleeve and showing me a fair approximation of his boss's signature rendered on his forearm with a soldering iron.

"Wow… Well anyway, you don't have to do this for me… but this girl came to town pregnant, and she says the Number One guy in your Master's favorite cult knocked her up, and she wants somebody to make it right. But the nutbags in the cult scooped her up and took her away, and I saw the celebrity resource center on the news, and she was there—"

"That's *impossible*. There *is* no Psylosophy celebrity center."

His eyes are bugged out in disbelief and, yes, *fear*. "It's a myth that people need to believe in, to get entirely unrelated shit done. It's like the basement at the Alamo, or the dead aliens in the trunk in *Repo Man*, or the briefcase—"

"That's what I'm saying! The news was coming from another LA, and that got me to thinking. Isn't that what the Psylosophy zombies are always saying? 'There's a universe next door where you've already won it all, and we have the key.' Wherever it is, that's where they took her."

"And why is it any business of yours?" Picking up the remote, he cranks the stereo.

"Wide Boy Awake. 'Chicken Outlaw.' Retarded one-hit New-Ro bullshit. Boy, 1982 sure was a shitty year for entertainment."

He turns around. "Get the fuck out of our house."

I back away. "Hey, I didn't mean anything by it. You're up here buying art student projects for your boss, so he can pretend to be some kind of polymath genius instead of just a depraved, soulless creep, that's your business. But I think the real creeps... the *other* creeps, who run this cult, are going to take the girl's baby away, or worse, and so naturally, it seemed to me your boss would either be interested in hearing that his messiah was about to come upon the earth... or he's one of the Pharisee douchebags who wants to smother the baby Psylosophy Jesus in his manger..."

I back up until I'm against the mirrored wall and can see the tangle of power strips and wall-warts at the far end of his desk. I kick all the plugs out of the wall. Everything goes dead. The stereo, the servers, the monitors, the ceiling fans—

I can still hear bass. When I kneel, I feel it tickling the palm of my hand through an ivory Berber carpet like Danish babies' hair. "What's in the basement at the Alamo, Kevin?"

TWENTY-TWO

[CUE: Ratatat, "Rome"; Nino Olivieri & Riz Ortolani, "Cargo Cult Finale" from *Mondo Cane*]

IT'S ALWAYS TOUGH FOR A NEW RELIGION. WHEN the people your messiah cuckolded, knocked up and ripped off are still alive and looking for a competent ghostwriter in their trauma support groups. When your secret, sacred teachings and your police record are available online for any infidel with a blog to play armchair theologian over.

And how much more difficult to be taken seriously, so long as anybody remembers that your religion was based on a parody of a cult everybody already hates?

You can search the net forever and you won't find video or even a rundown of the sketch that ran only once on an otherwise forgettable ripoff of *Saturday Night Live* and *In Living Color* that wanted to be more daring and obnoxious than its competitors, so it went after sacred cows, or at least a lot of targets that kneejerk sue anyone who criticizes them. They were canceled after five episodes.

The controversial mockumentary-style sketch profiled a human potential cult called Psylosophy, and its founder, Xavier Doderlik, a failed comedian who basically turned all his old workshop clichés into a religion that catered to other desperate failed actors and comics.

Dressed in the world's most expensive tuxedo T-shirt, he rails at his disciples, "You're Always ON. There's always an audience. The Devil is a heckler, and you must silence him with your best material!" Doderlik then uses his techniques to become the Devil, a baby, former heavyweight champion George Foreman and a platypus, then all four at once. It's a miracle.

The fictional cult takes Dianetics' secrecy fetish over the edge, with the very existence of the cult a litigable secret, and celebrities in vagina-pyramid hats denying any knowledge of or affiliation with the cult. In a clanky parody of the E-Meter, the Psylosophy initiate must successfully tickle himself and pin an audience meter with his desperate laughter into an electrified Mr. Microphone. Recruiters are pressured to bring fresh fish every day, but are shocked by remote whenever they publicly admit Psylosophy exists. No text or recordings of the master's lectures exist, so pledges must memorize speeches verbatim, causing them to lose their own memories and basic humanity and become gibbering human tape recorders.

Pretty forgettable stuff, if you're not a Scientologist or a lawyer. Though no malice aforethought was proven in court, the nuisance lawsuits persisted until the network let go of the young actor who wrote and portrayed Doderlik in the sketch. He tried to return to the club circuit and improv troupes, but nobody wants to book you when dead-eyed weirdos show up and catcall that you're a Nazi.

So your career is screwed and they seem to track you down every time you switch to a pseudonym, and they lie to all your friends about shit you did so you have nowhere to go, and nobody you can trust.

So you flee the land of your birth and move to the only country where your archenemies are illegal, and you scrape by as an English-language tour guide at Dachau, waiting for the heat to blow over, checking in with old friends from the Groundlings, and trying to recapture your dream of making people laugh.

But you're not feeling very funny, and nothing inspires you

anymore, except those whacko assholes who ruined your life for having the temerity to make fun of them. You record some new standup and send it to your few diehard friends and fans in the states, but it's all angry rants that slowly evolve into the tenets of Psylosophy, an endless, nasty, self-destructive joke that somehow catches on and becomes the joke that never stops telling you.

Somebody puts together a compilation of your rants and it makes the rounds of tape-traders and the early internet. The rants are laced with unsubtle demands for money, and people who should know better start sending you some. Then a lot. Then you start hearing about dorks in tuxedo t-shirts screaming Monty Python routines and Psylosophy slogans—"I want something for nothing, and I'll do anything to get it!"— at Travolta's movie premieres.

And when you have enough money and burnout American fanatics bumming around your Berlin studio to rekindle your long-dormant drug problem, you get an idea.

You apply to renew your expired US passport, and you incorporate the Unchurch of Psylosophy, using your new legal name: Xavier Doderlik.

It's a brilliant move, you brilliant motherfucker, you. High-five yourself!

In America, while freethinkers, atheists and God-botherers might live to piss on each other's shoes, there's no real percentage in religious enterprises going after each other. To sling mud at a rival faith only highlights that other faiths exist.

So long as you fleece your own suckers and pull the gospel out of your own ass, you can write your own ticket. The martyrdom, the days of struggle, are behind you. Your every idle impulse and perverse whim becomes holy writ to legions of overeducated underachievers who swiftly forget they were doing this on a goof, and if there aren't enough of them to add up to a proper church with a celebrity center, you can still afford to throw a party that never ever ends, moving from one famous patsy to the next, draining the cocaine, hors d'oeuvres and champagne reserves of every host until somebody drops dead, then starting over at the top of the donor roster.

But you prematurely ejaculated in Hef's grotto once already in your first incarnation of fame, and the earthly fruits of success, the kicks of playing Thulsa Doom of Malibu, wear off pretty fast. Like every gangster antihero in every *Scarface* ripoff you ever watched in German on fuzzy European cable, you succumb to the temptation of getting high on your own bullshit supply.

You lock yourself away for weeks, months, years, perfecting the cosmic improv techniques you've been touting as the key to self-invention, of acting out the life you want to live so convincingly that the universe breaks down and you slip into the reality you really belong in. You've started to believe you really can travel between realities at will, waking up in the bejeweled ruins of post-apocalyptic Malibu to frolic in the surf over sunken Santa Monica with the Eloi; going to the gladiator matches in a fascist dystopia and pigging out on cannibal buffet; then partying in orbit above a utopian now that never fought the Cold War or Vietnam or Desert Storm; and going to bed in the strangest world of all, where your stupid coked-out rants have become holy scripture more fiercely defended than the Koran or the Bible, and you are worshipped as a living god, and your luminous, smiling idol blocks out the sun over Hollywood until the first teamster coffee break every day. This last one is nice enough that you murder your doppelganger there and take his place.

Maybe these worlds you wander and conquer are real, and maybe they're the products of the drugs your fanatical followers and unscrupulous doctors provide on demand. Maybe you should have been less trusting of your lieutenants, or of the one great celebrity who went public with his devotion in that pushover LA next-door, and blew your covert cult up into the world's shiniest faith.

This former child-star burnout and rediscovered hot young box-office sensation admits that he owes everything to Psylosophy, that he manifested his success almost out of thin air by applying himself diligently to the warm-up and visualization techniques you perfected. He has not only brought his love for Psylosophy out of the closet, he has made it sound almost like a plausible faith, no more ridiculous in elite circles than Kabbalah or Pastafarianism or the Mormons.

But in your perennial interdimensional absences, the little shit has taken over everything. You're a prisoner in your beach compound, drugged and milked for countless hours of sleepwalking lectures that they sell on ridiculously expensive, self-destructing cassettes. You can't focus long enough to beg someone to help you, let alone will yourself into a kinder reality but one night several years later, you break free and light out in a used Itasca motorhome.

Cruising the desert highways of the Southwest, your mind gradually clears, and you rediscover the trick of hypnotizing yourself across time and space. You fell so in love with your rotten ego that you tried to change worlds, when the secret was to change yourself, to allow the role to rule, the changes to claim you.

Like a freewheeling fugitive from a mid-70's crime show, you roll from town to town in a million Americas, solving mysteries and sharing wisdom while getting young, attractive women everywhere pregnant with your mind-clouding prowess.

You made a mess of your life and in the process, stumbled upon a miracle. Now, too late to save yourself or the world you came from, you sow your seed as recklessly as you spread your word, hoping against hope that somewhere, in one or another of the countless Americas that have accepted your gold coins in lieu of cash and taken your shriveled but boundlessly charming carcass into their beds, a hero will someday rise and reclaim the hereditary wisdom of interdimensional travel through improvisational comedy from the depraved assholes who usurped your teachings.

And your guidance counselor said standup comedy was a waste of a life…

TWENTY-THREE

[CUES: Felix & His Fabulous Cats, "Savage Girl"; Enoch Light & The Light Brigade, "Temptation"]

HIS SHRUG IS THE PLATONIC IDEAL OF "uncomfortable," like being caught giving yourself a stranger at a funeral. "Don't go down there. You *can't* go down there."

"What's down there, Kev?"

"Just… some people are hanging out. It's an after-party."

"At Four o'clock. That's more like after the after-after party, isn't it…? Who's down there, Kev?"

"None of my business. So it's none of your business *cubed*."

I promise not to tell. Cross my heart. "Y'think TMZ would pay for an unsourced bit on your boy being an accessory to an extortion ring run by Blood Eagle Security?"

He takes off, pacing erratically but gradually easing himself through the sprawling house to the cellar door off the servants' kitchen. "That's not even remotely true, and those people are vicious thugs. How could you? Why would you…?"

I follow close behind, stepping over and stumbling around a giant, clear plastic ball with an all-too lifelike Richard Pryor dummy suspended in it, and that retarded robot dog from the original *Battlestar Galactica*. "If it were true, nobody would care. They'd keep it a secret because it'd be like Night of the Living Pellicanos, and half the village would burn down, if he started talking about what he'd seen and done. But who cares? If people *want* it to be true, and your guy is ripe for another scandal…"

"God damn it, Charlie…" He stops in the kitchen and leans against the replacement for the massive glass table I broke last Xmas, when Kevin and his boss were in Reykjavik. "I swear, he's not a member. It's true, what people always say, you know… He'd never join a cult that wouldn't let him worship himself. They just rent the basement when he's away… He's too proud to admit it, but he's not drawing a tenth of what they say he's getting in the trades. Cocksucking parasites. The studios have him by the balls after the last time he—"

"What's down there…?" I point at the door. I've been down there before, and it's just a normal wine cellar down there, with a pretty pedestrian collection of mostly novelty vinegar with celebrity vanity vineyard labels, and a few thousand-dollar bottles of expensive French piss that didn't taste half as good as the two-buck Chuck Kevin and I replaced it with. (OK. …that *I* replaced it with. Still did him a favor.)

Kevin runs his hands through his hair, tugs it until his eyes bug out, then sits on his hands. "No names."

"What?"

He goes over and takes out a key, unlocks the cellar door and steps back like it might fly open. "Whatever happens, you can't drop a single name. Not one, and not even a blind item oral account of anything you see down there, not even to yourself in the fucking bathtub or they'll know, and they'll come for me, and you'll have the life expectancy of a vegan steamer at Southie Batman's house."

"*A… what?*" I go to the door and open it. The dim orange light reveals the wine, and obscures the hidden passage in the back of the cellar, but I can see the false-wall door is wide open on another flight of stairs. Dug out under the property by some specially-selected contractors who did time for excavating a half-mile drug tunnel from TJ to San Ysidro that stayed undiscovered for eighteen years.

"You're a good friend," I tell him.

"I wish I could say the same," he says. He's got something behind his back.

"Oh, for fuck's sake." I set foot on the first step. I've never been past the door that Kevin once told me goes under the next two properties to a fuckpad deluxe once owned by W_____ B_____ and L____ S_____. "Give it here."

He hands me the mint-condition hardcover copy of *Spoiled Rotten* and a pen. Looks over my shoulder as I scribble in it. "No. Your *real* name."

I scratch out my signature and give him the book. "Happy now?"

He tucks the book under one arm, zips up his Members Only jacket and snaps that collar strap thing that *nobody* ever actually uses. "I'm good enough of a friend to trust you this far. But I'm not a good enough friend to go down with you, and I never saw you before. I don't know how you got down there. Don't try to come up this way. It'll be locked."

Kevin closes the door in my face.

Nowhere to go but down…

[CUE: Amon Tobin w/ Kid Koala, "Untitled" mashed with whale song, Apollo 11 moon landing chatter; Mozart, "Piano Concerto no. 21 in C Major" Squeeze, "Take Me, I'm Yours"]

Blacklights everywhere make it clear the omnipresent milky stains are nothing to be ashamed of. Radiating glamour is more than just not smelling like sewage. Legendary sweat, immortal butt-cheese musk, the skidmarks of demigods, glisten on every surface.

I've seen these pictures in my dreams. I've burned for them all my life.

The music gets louder, but I don't see anybody. It's not even dark out, but this is the after-after-afterparty that was the afterparty to the afterparty to a party in continuous effect, so legend would have it, since New Year's in Aspen, 2002.

The hallway ends at a big room lit only by Moroccan lamps swaddled in burgundy gauze and syrupy incense smoke.

Soft red walls. frankincense and burning semen. Four rows of heavily padded couches with IV stands are parked in the room. A perfect naked body lies on every one, with goggles over their eyes out of which leak pulses of spectral light. Attendants in burqas and veils massage feet and temples, palpate and prick flaccid, chafed genitals with gold needles. A rail-thin musician wrings a creeping pulse out of a percussion pad and coaxes weird shuddery sounds out of a Theremin, cementing the vibe of a vampires' rehab ward in a whale's womb.

All is stillness and peace.

A door opens and I crouch behind the nearest couch and try not to be starstruck. J—— motherfucking H—— reclines beside me, emitting breathless meeping noises as all manner of pharmaceutical byproducts ooze from his screaming pores. A fresh, steaming body, redolent of milk and honey, is led to a couch and gently laid down and licked clean by a pair of identical twins, then swaddled in towels of raw silk. An attendant lurches over and fixes up the IV needle, jabs it into the inside of the right elbow, then pulls it out and tries again and again, like he's knitting. Suddenly, the body on the couch sits up ramrod straight and grabs the attendant's wrist and bends it back, twisting the hand to try to spike the guy's eye with the syringe.

"ARE YOU TRYING TO FUCKING KILL ME? LOOK AT ALL THOSE FUCKING BUBBLES IN THE LINE, YOU MORON!" The guy on the couch kicks the attendant in the chest and falls backwards, moaning, "Head rush," then whips around and points at me. "You. Are you straight?"

I tell him that depends who's asking.

"I don't want to fuck you. Are you in the K-hole with this other idiot?"

The attendant sinks under the couch, drooling.

I tell him I'm good.

"Then get off your goldbricking ass and spike me."

Takes me a second to sort out. "I don't wanna."

"What?"

I tell him I don't like needles.

"Fuck you, get over here. This other asshole, he could be an assassin from Fox, for all I know. He tried to fucking vapor-lock my line, and he couldn't even find the vein." He flexes a gnarly orange arm so hard that blood squirts from it like leaks in a garden hose. "LOOK AT THIS DEFINITION! Who couldn't find a vein in this ownage? Fucking amateur put so many holes in me, I could play 'El Condor Pasa' on my arm like a fucking flute. I don't know how many of these fuckers he spiked, but half of CBS's fall line-up probably just got cancelled, THANK YOU VERY LITTLE!"

He tries to get up to kick the attendant and swoons again. He's like a hundred-fifty pounds of shrink-wrapped orange licorice. No fat, no hair, nothing but gnarled muscle under traffic-cone skin that twitches on his jumpy skeleton. "Fucking relax, fucker," he mutters to himself. "Fucking *Namaste*." Cracked-out for days, but he still seems like the sharpest tool I've pulled from the drawer all day. And he thinks I work here.

I help him back to his couch and punch up his pillow. Hair chicken-fried and bleached to pieces, sticking out in brittle Glazer-Fieri stalagmites that crunch like pork rinds when he lies back on the couch and closes his eyes.

I take the needle. His vein is a jumpy nightcrawler, a baby garter snake squirming under livid skin. I trap it and prick it and squeeze the bag to get the solution going. "What's in here?"

"Propietary formula." He chuckles. "Life Juice."

It sure looks like blood. I look at the label on the bag. It says LIFE JUICE™.

"Fucking B__ fucking A_____ had a coronary at daybreak, and my juice brought him back, word to fuckin' pimp. Whacked on enough Russian military-grade MDMA to turn Pyongyang into Amsterdam, and he just started sucking off every guy who came up, and baby-birding the cum into M___ D____'s mouth and then S_____ came over and they 69'd for like an hour while J_____ R_____ rubbed his pitiful micropenis in their hair and K____ S_____ jacked off and took Polaroids, and it was like, the most beautiful thing, like when you look off your deck and see a mule deer with her fawn, and you pin them together with a single crossbow bolt, and she runs away on pure adrenaline with her baby pinned to her side. Like you took this beautiful thing and *bent* it, you know?

"So he comes out of it, and he's got this shit-eating grin, like literally, he's a big-time fecal freak, I can't blame his wife for kicking him out, you know he had a special toilet that stored people's poop in a trap so he could munch it later... No *shit*, heh.

"So, anyway, he's staggering around and somebody gives him a cocoa puff and he looks like the ghost of R_____ E____, which is trippy, because E___ is alive and getting a Cleveland steamer from C___ T____ on the next couch."

"Awful lot of poo play," I blurt out, "for a celebrity gala."

"You don't play *pee* games in the Poop Game room, little man. So he's racing around like a hummingbird and then he just keels over, so we spike him, and the aestheticians go to work, and the paramedic ices his rectum, and no thanks to some people," he throws a sandal at the attendant, lovingly fellating somebody's toes, "we brought him back. Xmas is saved a month early, it's a godfucking damn miracle."

Pause for applause.

"He just sits bolt upright and belts out a maniacal laugh and says he just had the most incredible idea for a screenplay, like a lightning bolt, and this time, he's going to win an Oscar for his *own* writing, and he storms off to do that shit. Bitch better thank me, or at least give Life Juice a shout-out... Shit ain't easy to make, man. If you know how to get Mormon children's blood fresh from Salt Lake, fuck, I don't care..."

"What was the idea?"

"Which one? The screenplay? Some bullshit, who cares... You're kind of a pain in the ass, who invited you?"

I open the Life Juice shunt until he passes out, and before I leave the room, the K-hole attendant has crawled over to suck on my new buddy's toes, and all is forgiven.

I sneak down a long, dim hall lined with closed doors. I gently twist a couple but find them locked, and then, for my sins, one of them opens. I look inside, and I scream so hard that my soul tries to escape out my open mouth.

Ever heard of the Order of Napoleons?

Of course you haven't. Even if you're in the biz, where people talk incessantly about nothing but the industry and each other, you could go a hundred years without running into anyone who irresponsible enough to know and share such scurrilous filth, at least not with names attached. But within the outermost circles of Hollywood society, there persists a rumor about a tiny but ruthless cabal that has quietly controlled the three biggest studios in Hollywood and ruined more careers than cocaine in the process.

So some asshole producer throws a Come As You Were party in 1978, when reincarnation and past lives were a fad between pet rocks and pyramid schemes. It's like a funny kind of personality test, one bored junior studio manager observes to a colleague as they snort teaspoons of coke by the pool at a palace in the Hills. A lot of actors showed up as Billy the Kid, Marc Antony, Hercules or the Lone Ranger. The starlets and wanna be's were all Cleopatra, Joan of Arc, or Mata Hari, and more than a couple missed the whole point adorably by coming as Marilyn Monroe.

More illuminating than that, retorts his colleague, *Look at us*, and they both laughed, for they were both dressed as Napoleon.

As the night drags on, they winnow out two more Napoleons, including a brassy chick who packaged two of ABC's highest-rated shows. They withdraw into another room with a couple models to get royally fucked up on coke and champagne and come up with some sort of insane notion that they really ARE all Napoleon.

Do a big fat line of your kid's ADD meds and meet me in the next graph.

OK.

So just suppose that God never intended for there to be this many of us. Clearly, the Bible doesn't have all the answers. Jesus, careful reading of Scriptures tells us, believed and insisted that he would return bearing a sword within the lifetimes of the people who witnessed his life and crucifixion. Which is why Christians have been pissed to find themselves not extinct for going on two thousand years. And we are long overdue for the asswhipping of Kali Yuga, a period of catastrophic upheaval foretold in the Sanskrit scriptures, in which humanity turns to its nadir of spiritual development and blows itself up. That was supposed to start happening in 3100 BC.

So maybe reincarnation works, but souls divide when children are born from the finite reserve allotted by God and/or nature. Sure, they backfilled, snorting lines out the cleavage of a comatose Penthouse Pet, that's why people don't live 700 years like Noah in the Bible, why everybody is a lazy, craven idiot instead of badasses like the knights of Medieval Europe or Samurai-era Japan. Because the world is the same batch of old souls, spread thinner over more bodies, every generation. Who knows how many bodies the soul of Napoleon currently occupies, they wonder, but together, they feel more than just the kinship of like-minded sociopaths on top-grade drugs. They feel like one tiny, brilliant little motherfucker, his pitiful one-inch wiener a blessing that spared him the temptations of ordinary flesh, and vouchsafed for him a mighty destiny.

So would the four of them pledge to unite and serve each other's interests as their own in all things, and thereby conquer Hollywood.

Everybody else forgot that party, but the four Napoleons never did, nor did they forget the other would-be conquerors at the party—the bookish director who came as Julius Caesar, the lecherous record producer who came as Rasputin; the dowdy bitch of a talent manager who came as Queen Elizabeth. Working together in their respective studios, they traded scripts and talent and favors, and swiftly rose through the ranks until, by the end of the Eighties, each of them was either running a studio or holding the vomit dish for the doomed fucker nominally in charge.

By then, Julius Caesar was a whoremongering drunk and a laughingstock; the record producer was nailed for statutory rape while visiting a state where they make it stick, due to an anonymous tip; and Queen Elizabeth committed suicide after her entire client list was mailed tapes of phone conversations about them behind their backs. (And all three of the unfortunate girls who came as Marilyn Monroe had found some success only to die under tragic, mysterious circumstances hastily ruled as suicide by police. History doesn't repeat here, it just stutters.)

By the early 90's, the Napoleons were starting to get old and out of touch, having blown a fortune in the notorious framed wood Ponzi scheme, and the endless excess began to take a real toll. None of them wanted to end up like Don Simpson. But their grip was slipping.

It must've been the same one who came up with the reincarnation idea in the first place. They would each be stronger, he reasoned, snorting a gray-market brain-enhancing product in his Malibu hot tub, if the Napoleon energy were not spread so thinly. The other Napoleon in the hot tub at the time agreed, and they proceeded to decide which of the others should be sacrificed.

How it went down varies from telling to telling, but by the millennium, there were three Napoleons, and between them, they controlled 76% of the filmed entertainment in theaters and 13% of TV.

And right now, the three of them are naked on the floor in a daisy chain that makes *Human Centipede* look like *The Sound Of Music*.

Bicorne hat askew, squishy yellow shit smeared all over his face except for his lips, so he looks like some kind of coprophiliac minstrel show performer, one of them looks up and bellows, "*You're not the boy*! SEND US THE BOY!"

"Right away, boss," I say, and close the door.

Somebody throws an arm around my throat, crushing my trachea like a cheap straw. Husky voice whispers, "Where d'you think you're going, little bitch?" Somebody else rudely takes my pants down and starts sobbing into my crotch.

Gasping for breath. Slammed into the wall. And in spite of my best efforts, sporting a boner.

Call it conditioning, but even I can't resist the siren song of the former queen of hardcore porn when she starts hyperventilating, *Get it, Daddy,* in my ear as she batters my ass with a strap-on, growling and humping her pubic arch against my tailbone. I can't make myself limp, even with her husband, the former UFC heel, on his knees in front of me, singing to it. I want to ask how they're doing, the tabloids abuzz with their domestic problems, but it's clear they're in couples' therapy and doing just great.

"I got places to be," I tell my new friends.

"Not until my bitch is done with you," J____ growls. "Do you like your new chew-toy, bitch?"

Her husband lubes my pubes with his tears and vehemently nods.

"Being as awful as a man won't win you back your dignity, hon. And you…" I tap her husband's head. "Being a dog now won't win back her respect. Just don't hit her next time, okay?"

She looks me in the eye like she's going to spit at me, and then her pupils seem to drink me in with something approaching awe. "Thank you, master," she says, and her estranged husband prays to my penis.

A perfectly built, massive naked man comes out of a room waist-deep in soap suds and gently lifts the ultimate fighter off my groin. It's A_____ S_____, or a remarkable simulation. Naked except for a sheer mask that emits an HD image of the Governator's rigorously scanned face. It looks just convincing enough to be creepy, even above and beyond the current context, like the weird singing headstones in Disney's Haunted Mansion.

A similarly attired female usher comes for J_____, her mask emitting a flickering B_____ P____ likeness, but she resists and her voice drops five octaves. I'm not ready to switch back! I'm having a breakthrough!" This couple's therapy is more radical that I gave it credit for.

She slaps the attendant hard, harder, hardest and each time the mask pixelates and resolves into a different celebrity visage. She keeps slapping until the usher's mask looks like G____ J____ and then woozily staggers off on her arm, wading into the foam room.

I creep down the hall. Hear someone talking, loud, unmistakable coke-jag cadence. I can't peek around the not-quite shut door, but I recognize the voice of the fourth most powerful agent in Hollywood.

"They always come up and they ask me that: *How do I become a star?* It's the second stupidest question they ever ask. If you don't see it when you look in the mirror, if you don't feel it eating you alive every minute you're not in the limelight, then you will never, ever get there.

"It's not a question of looks, or drive, or, God fucking forbid, talent. There's that quality, that something that lets people take you into their hearts as fantasy boyfriend, imaginary dad, sweet little sister, or the Devil. And you can't get it, you'll never discover it in a workshop. We tell people it's an indefinable magical Factor X, but we all know that's bullshit. Stars aren't born, they're bent. You can't teach or learn it, but you can create it.

"Just have a child. Work with them from the moment they can see you clearly. When your face is the sun and the moon, teach them how to act, to associate your love with the effort of performance.

"You don't have to take them to auditions and talent scouts from early childhood. If you do that, you'll burn them out by puberty. You don't want to raise a *child star*, trust me.

"If you neglect them, they'll grow up so hungry for attention they'll clamp onto the first person who takes an interest and get themselves trapped under a marriage and children. If you want that, breed puppies. You don't want pets that outlive you.

"And for the love of God, don't actually molest them. Time was, not a single beautiful girl came to Hollywood without some handsy stepdad, uncle, neighbor or drama teacher spoiling them for anything but softcore, if they had any gifts at all besides a good gag reflex. They self-destruct if you try to

CODY GOODFELLOW

take something that broken inside to the highest stratosphere of fame. But the world needs strippers, too…

"You have to rehearse every scene with them and take them through the Doderlik method. You have to do *Romeo And Juliet* with them and be their first love and kill and die with them, take their first kiss over and over until they do it right. Take them through the heights of love, passion, lust and death in endless rehearsals, and you have utterly destroyed their emotional virginity without spoiling their physical innocence. Disney understood this, from A_____ F_____ and B_____ S_____ to K___ R_____ and R___ G_____, they understood how to tame songbirds without clipping their wings.

"If you know where to look, you can hire coaches who'll put your kids through that kind of rigorous quantum drama abuse, but if you want to be sure of their star quality, you have to tend and ripen the fruit yourself, never tasting it, but deepening its sweetness by banking the fires of its life force. By the time they go to their first audition, they've experienced every human emotion to the hilt, known love and loss, and yet they're incapable of *feeling* those things, except when they pretend.

"And that, my friends, is how stars are made."

The group applauds and when the noise dissolves into a mush of murmuring, I hear another voice out of many that makes me say, *Fuck this sneaking shit*, throw open the door and stride in most commandingly.

It's quite an entrance, but no one seems to notice. Murky green sunlight, filtered through a swimming pool. A whole wall on the far end is Plexiglas, like the viewing window into a Shamu tank, but the pool is olive green, cloudy with filth, the slimy surface swarming with paddling ducks.

I push through curtains of smoke, clouds of agents and executives in matching monogrammed robes, each smoking a cigarette or a vape rig with one hand and stroking a blind, pop-eyed teacup Chihuahua with the other, claw and scratch and shove to get at the one person here I feel comfortable screaming at.

"Some kind of weather we're having, eh, Mimi?"

She sits in a wicker chair in a corner beside the submarine picture window. One of her hairless greyhound things brings her a mai tai. She says something, but the murmur and rasp of the other conversations drowns her out.

I ask her if we can go somewhere private to talk, not wanting to embarrass her in front of the most powerful power brokers who ever broke power.

"I'm going to need the room," Mimi bellows, and without a single moan, the whole crowd falls silent and faces the opposite wall. Only plumes of cigar smoke move in the stifling stillness.

"I, uh, didn't think you carried that much weight in the industry. You know, judging by *my* career…"

"You're given no more and no less than you need, Shinobi."

"Don't call me that."

"But that's your name. Your *real* name. You were great, once. If only you could stop running from what you were, and be what you could be… If you could just see the larger plan, you'd understand everything that's happened has been for his highest good."

"Who's *he*? Doderlik?"

Her dog slaps me. Paw like a catcher's mitt whips my head around and slams me into the plexiglass wall.

I sink into a chair, massaging a bruised cheek. "So you're one of them."

Mimi looks elaborately hurt. "Do you need to know *all* my private business? I protect your secrets well enough."

"My secrets don't secretly control Hollywood, hon. So you knew about the whole thing with the girl, with the baby… Where is she? At the Celebrity Center?"

"This is it, dummy. This *is* the celebrity center, in this reality. It's kind of an interdimensional floater, and to be frank, it's been here way too long. Compared to the other realities, the franchise here is a joke. In our universe, the Headliner died a broke nobody. This reality failed him. All the lecture tapes

CODY GOODFELLOW

he recorded come from a parallel universe, so at least there's a good reason why ours are so expensive…

"You should see the records archive. The complete works of the Headliner, plus all the financial and personnel stuff and blackmail material. It's all stashed in this crazy cat lady's Subaru, so no one can make a subpoena stick. Four hundred thousand miles on it, and it's like her fifth car…"

"So why is that guy here?" I point at the fourth biggest agent in America.

"We lowered our standards," she says. "But the ones who really matter, you'll never know."

"I know everybody," I say, and she smirks. "I know *of* everybody," I amend.

"That guy over there… He used to be a screenwriter." In spite of that, I recognize his name. If it had a number in the title and was a piece of shit, chances are he wrote it, about ten years ago. If I had to speculate, I figure he'd be teaching his obsolete, shopworn take on the craft to wannabe's in UCLA Extension classes, but here he is, at the center of a wheel of other wall-eyed, cracked-out insiders.

"He moved up to the big leagues." Mimi lowers her voice to a ridiculous stage whisper. "Consensus engineering."

"What?"

"He writes the news."

"And again… what?"

"D_____," Mimi says, and like a clockwork president, the screenwriter starts talking like when he stops, he'll drop dead.

"They accuse us of doing it all the time, anyway… Waco, 9/11, all those school shootings, the fucking moon landing… and they busted education down so bad, people couldn't follow anything smarter than a Punch & Judy show, unless it's a movie, and then all the sudden, they're astute critics of veracity.

"We don't have to shape their reality. We just keep on making the reality they'd rather live in.

"Because movies tell stories. The news just goes on and on,

fuzzy with details and contradictions and the cowards always let the assholes win… but stories, they have heroes and villains, and a beginning and an end.

"For every downer news story, we shit out an Oscar-bait issue melodrama for adults and a dystopian soap opera for the kids, where good triumphs and justice is served, and nobody even Googles to see who really won.

"Once we replaced the news, there was only one place to go… Reality TV was a battle to the death, and reality lost. Overnight, we found we could spin a whole new American mythology to keep the lumpen proles sleeping soundly in their toxic waste trailers, thinking all was right in the world.

"And if the fucks back east don't protect our copyrights in China this year, we'll bury them in unhappy endings and the flyover state peasants will wake up and smell the frack-piss in their drinking water, and maybe someday actually revolt."

The whole room cackles until it coughs up black blood.

"Shut up," she says, and he does. She turns to look at me. "Oh, stop with the victim eyes. Nobody who likes to sleep at night ever wants to know how these things go down."

I can tell her she's evil, but she's hardly wrong. Sure it sucks, but at least it's a system. Pretty much every dance and R&B hit after 1978 was chosen by an autistic black giant (6'11", 190lbs.) who rollerskated up and down the promenade between Trader Vic's and the fountain at the Wilshire-Santa Monica crossroads every day from 7 to 7. Some said he was the fucked-up son of some dead crooner, and nobody ever knew where he went when he wasn't skating round the damn fountain. The music he enjoyed on a ghetto blaster and later a Walkman was slipped to him by junior execs at Capitol, A&M, Warner and the rest, and didn't reach the general public unless it made the big freak groove. Dropped dead of an aneurysm in the summer of '92, which is why shit like the Spin Doctors and Limp Bizkit happened.

"So what's the deal with the girl… You're gonna have the Brentwood Illuminati here just scrape her, shoot her and bury her in the Hills, or what?"

"You should forget her. I know you better than that, but still. You think you're doing this for her, but you don't know her. You're doing it for how she makes you feel…"

Finally, an argument I can kick the shit out of. "Nobody does anything *for* anyone. People who help other people do it because it feels *good*, right? Nobody would help anyone if it made them feel shitty, would they? Unless they *like* to feel shitty, and then there you are, again.

"What I mean is, Nobody can ever really *know* anybody else, so what's the point? You do what makes you feel good. Bad people, good people, everybody's just doing what feels right, right? You love the way someone makes you feel. You love someone so they'll love you back. She makes me feel like I can help somebody, and I know it's because I can't help myself… but I feel like I can help her. And that feels good like I haven't felt in longer than I can remember."

"That's not very long at all. Come on, Shinobi."

Mimi makes a shy *psst* sound that slices through the room. The fourth-biggest agent in Hollywood comes over.

"This is him," Mimi says.

He looks me over, cutting up my face with his eyes. "I didn't see it before, but yeah. If he's down with the master plan, we could make some heat, baby."

"We? Like… *me*…?" I choke on my spit.

"Hell yes." He puts a hand on my shoulder. "My doctor tells me I can have all the jelly donuts I want, if I just suck the filling out and put the pastry back in the box." Stoops into my space and sucks up my smell with a meaty, greedy nose. "But I'd like to take a bite of you, son."

His breath has no odor whatsoever.

"Gosh, this is all so…" *fucking creepy*? Strangers offering to monetize your sex appeal sounded infinitely better before it actually happened.

"It's long overdue. Especially if you come clean about

before. The backlash is over, so bring on the re-lash, says I. We were talking earlier about some of your story ideas, man."

This is the seduction I've waited my entire life for. I just wish I could comprehend it. "Are you offering to represent me, or option my story concepts?"

"Yeah!" the agent says. "Mimi told me a few of the more marketable ones. You should totally get those down on paper. You're sitting on solid gold. Particularly the one about the fecal people... I love that shit, *heh heh*..."

I just nod at him, grinning fixedly until Mimi tells him to screw off for a minute. "You *still* have a problem?"

"You've been sending me to babysit old women and beat people with their own dogs for how many years now, and the day I find out about this girl, suddenly..."

"You thought hard work and a positive attitude were what opened doors in this town?"

"NO, but... if this group is so powerful, how come you live in a trailer under a bridge? How come you never worked like this for me before...?"

"Real power doesn't need to announce itself everywhere. Our motto, There's an infinite number of worlds where you're winning. Pick one. All you have to do to stay is kill the version of you who lives there. Hollywood isn't a town of winners, it's a refugee camp of kicked dogs, runaways, fat kids, bitter dreamers and self-loathing wanna-be messiahs, so you have to play the underdog, if you want to stay on top."

I look around. They're all looking at me like I matter more than they're comfortable with. Like I'm key evidence in a high-profile murder trial. I imagine my shit-people movie franchise clogging multiplex toilets around the world. "Where is she? I want answers!"

Mimi sighs. "*Still* with the adolescent bullshit?"

"Hey, credit where credit is due, this morning you said I was being infantile. That's a whole lot of growth in one day."

Everybody loses interest and turns away to watch the

ducks. "I'm not Dr. Exposition, asshole. You want answers, there's someone who loves the sound of his own voice as much as you do, who'll be thrilled to hear you insisted on doing this the hard way."

I turn around to see if he's here, and walk right into a blackjack wielded by Mimi's prize Valhalla's Celtic Lurck, Xerxes.

TWENTY-FOUR

[Cue: DJ Food, "The Crow"]

EVERYONE WHO EVER GOT CRUSHED TRYING TO make it in this town, who ever concluded that the world was rigged to make them suffer and die a nobody… They don't know how easy they have it.

Because even the least distinguished loser in the back of the bus has more of a chance than someone who made it once, and then fucked it up.

When nobody knows anything, the stink of failure is fatal. They never stop forgiving you if you keep making them money, but the minute they see nothing worth saving but a loyal, desperate friend, you're dead.

(And now for the least surprising reveal of the new fall season.)

Shinobi Honeycutt? That evil scene-stealing, butt-invading, parent-suing, prepubescent impregnator of beloved sitcom moms?

He's me.

That's my real name.

(Seriously, don't pretend to be surprised. Bro, do you even *Fight Club*?)

I got too famous too fast and I freaked out hard, then freaked out harder when they cut me off. I went away. I grew up and tried to just live my life, tried to reconnect with the love of performing.

The best gig I ever had in show business, they put you into the suit and then they knock on your cock. It's no more personal or erotic than the cup check before a little league baseball game, when the umpire goes down the lineup at each dugout and verify the integrity of the unwieldy Tupperware strapped over your unripe plums.

This is to weed out the perverts. Furries get all pissy that their culture is reduced to a cheap joke, but in the shrinking pool of acceptable targets for mainstream mockery, they're the new mimes. So long as you're not sporting wood when you go into the arena, they can't say a thing.

In my time, I was Clifford, Cookie Mouse, Lyle Crocodile, the Cat In The Hat and the lead Wild Thing at public libraries, children's hospitals and battered women's shelters. The bigger the head, the baggier the padding, the better the encounter will go, when you're done frolicking and acting out the story and the children are allowed to come and hug you.

When their sticky hands clutch you and their juice-stained faces mash against you, their small soft feverish bodies squirming over you like blind newborn kittens on their exhausted mother, drinking from the teat of dreams, from which pure love flows.

There's always one kid a year too old for story time who climbs over the other kids to peer into the mesh eyes of your animal head. They always crow, "I can see a *man* in there!" If you can hurt this kid or shut him up without disturbing the rest of the group, you may help save the future.

But one day, I came out in the Cookie Mouse outfit, and instead of the squee and screech of ecstatic kids, I was blinded by flashbulbs and buffeted and wrestled to the ground by reporters who unmasked me like a Scooby Doo villain.

TROUBLED CHILD STAR NOW SERIAL TOT GROPER, said the headlines. Not one complaint before they found out who I had been, but once you have to say, "I never touched them," you're already dead. Get yourself buried.

I couldn't hide, so I went away again. I was finally going

to kill myself when Mimi cold-called me and offered me a deal. She believed I was a talented actor who deserved a second chance. If I'd put myself in her hands, she'd rebuild my career from scratch. She paid for the Mexican plastic surgery, the new name and ID and everything… and then she booked me in the shittiest gigs the entertainment industry has to offer.

It was garbage and I would've given up and gone home if I had one, if not for the chance, every once in a while, to see Shirley. She didn't recognize me and if she did, she'd freak, flashing on the time I sexually assaulted her, trying to make her breast-feed me at the wrap party. But she loves the role I filled once, and is so far gone that sometimes, when her meds are way off, Mimi books me to come visit her, and lets me complain like it's the worst job I've ever done.

CODY GOODFELLOW

TWENTY-FIVE

[Cue: Kava Kon, "Piper of the Tongan Harvest"]
[SFX: Distant gunfire, sirens, dogs howling, light musical theater rehearsals.]

I'M IN THE PASSENGER SEAT OF THE MEAN librarian's Subaru. The dog didn't knock me out the first three times it sapped me, but I played along so he'd stop.

At least I don't need to ask her where we're going, because whatever else is wrong with the LA outside, at least one thing is pretty obvious right away.

Psylosophy is a lot bigger here than back home, in my LA. The *real* one—

If you come to Los Angeles to see stars, there's only one place you're certain to find and spend some quality time with the titans of show business.

Founded in 1906 by Dr. Hubert Eaton as an alternative to "unsightly, depressing stoneyards," the Forest Lawn family of cemeteries swiftly expanded from Glendale to the backside of Hollywood and four other southland locations. Rolling, sculpted hills, lush green lawns, plashing fountains, tasteful memorial architecture; a cast of thousands, from Gene Autry to George Zucco; and an art museum featuring the world's largest mounted religious painting, an original Bouguereau and the only *moai* ever "liberated" from Easter Island. Only three miles away, Forest Lawn Hollywood Hills also offers the Court of Liberty, featuring the nation's largest single continuous mosaic, the Lincoln Terrace and the Plaza of Mesoamerican Heritage. A tasteful afternoon of culture and beauty, sure to delight and comfort your bereaved friends and loved ones.

Spellbinding stuff, and even more so while watching the mean librarian hold the toy raygun to her temple and pump the trigger, irradiating her brain to stimulate recall or free cerebral wifi, or maybe trying to blow her brains out so she can stop talking like a zombie tourguide.

As we come put-putting up over the hills on the 2 and drop onto Interstate 5, the night sky is all but blocked by a gargantuan, luminous apparition of a man standing with one foot planted in Forest Lawn—Hollywood Hills, and the other in Forest Lawn—Glendale, three miles away. Even with his oversized feet a little awkwardly far apart in an all-too-intentional nod to Michelangelo's David, the pale, green-white marble statue thrusts some six miles into the sky, looking to the south with a stormy glare that makes Moses look like Gumby. A string of jets queuing up to land at Burbank Airport circle around his beltline like gnats.

"Impressive, isn't it?" the mean librarian says.

It takes nearly a minute to pass out from under the eclipse of its ass, another to escape its conspicuously enhanced bulge. "It can't be real," I say.

"Oh, it's real, alright. Real expensive, real fussy, real temperamental when the lenses get dusty, and the smoke and rain mess up the resolution. He takes up more power than the rest of the goddamn city, and the servers just to render the blessed thing... lordy, don't get me started."

It's a hologram, but still impressive. If they have a space program here, the astronauts can see him from orbit.

We turn off the 5 onto Atwater, cruising past burnt-out storefronts packed with raccoon-eyed refugees and ululating pilgrims. Clad in rags or cloaks made from outdated headshots stapled together, wrapped like mummies in magnetic tape and castoff costumes from the countless porno archive warehouses in the neighborhood. All the world's wanna-be's have come here to starve in his shadow, and in this world, there's nothing left but wanna-be's.

In a smarmy tour-guide tone, she explains, "When the Master finally died, his highest acolyte decreed that one grave would not be enough to contain his greatness... so he had the Master's remains divided and separately interred in tombs in each of the Forest Lawn locations. This entitled us to expand the memorials into welcome centers to comfort the bereaved, and eventually, we had the lawyers pull an eminent domain claim, and took over all the cemeteries. He could keep his office anywhere, but he still insists on staying close to the final resting place of the Master's head."

We approach a checkpoint at the cemetery gates—trucks mounted with machineguns, signs warning of minefields and a platoon of boys in undertaker's garb surround us with greaseguns cocked and loaded.

The mean librarian brandishes her toy raygun and hisses at them. They scramble out of our path and open the gates.

The dystopia ends at the fence. Beyond, the gentle rise of deep green turf and the tiered, wedding cake appearance of the hillside is exactly as it always was. The headstones and mausoleums gleam in the reflected glow of the colossal foot that sprouts from the neo-Gothic cathedral at the peak of the hill.

We park outside the cathedral, which is just a fancy shell for the enormous hologram projectors blasting the image of Doderlik so brightly that the mean librarian gives me a pair of those nearly opaque sunglasses with the cardboard arms they give you after an ophthalmology exam. The underside of his foot hovers over us, large enough to crush all of Forest Lawn and the surrounding zip code like a well-landscaped anthill.

We cross the street to enter an arcade of obelisks arranged around a mighty statue in Carrara marble of Xavier Doderlik, obviously the model for the monstrosity teabagging the entire county. At the back of the plaza, a smallish Baroque mausoleum that looks like a genuine antique. The librarian tells me they brought it over from Pere Lachaise stone by stone, after kicking some famous dead Parisian out of it.

The mean librarian pushes open the gates. We step into a crypt that is also a loading elevator. The gates close and we descend into the celebrity-saturated earth.

At the bottom, the mean librarian opens another gate and we cruise into a huge white marble room with a massive swimming pool like the Roman Pool at Hearst Castle. Hot chicks from Central Casting do the Australian crawl across the bottom in jeweled thongs in a hypnotic Esther Williams pattern, but never, ever come up for air.

A man in a blinding white suit stands at the edge of the pool with his back to us. When he finishes peeing, he tosses his champagne glass and turns to face me.

"Well, there's a plot twist I should've seen coming," I say to myself, because that's who I'm looking at, in that devastatingly handsome white suit.

Myself.

TWENTY-SIX

I GOT NOTHING.

Turn the fucking page already!

TWENTY-SEVEN

[CUE: Orbital, "Serious Pet Shop" from *Pusher* (2012) Soundtrack; Ennio Morricone, "Tue-Barbe Hunts Maynard" from *The Island* (1980) Soundtrack]

THIS TIME, YOU'RE ENTITLED TO BE SURPRISED, if not outraged and confused. This whole huge, squishy narrative turd has been circling a narcissistic singularity from the moment you flushed.

What would you do if you met yourself? Not some test-tube clone version of you, but the ultimate, perfect YOU, the idealized incarnation of you if you'd caught all the breaks, if you somehow came out on top?

I go to shake his hand, but when he takes it, I'm totally gonna flip him—

The mean librarian zaps me in the kidneys with the raygun. I go wobbly for a second before I remember it's just a crazy lady pointing a toy at me.

This other, much better-put-together me recoils like I'm made of kryptonite and young-country music. "Don't touch me!"

"So..." I gather my breath, "if we touched, would we both just explode, or would this whole universe shatter because of our identical particles interacting, or whatever?"

"I don't know," he shrugs. "I just don't want you fucking *touching* me."

I wouldn't want to touch me, either. I smell my breath, and it's rancid. Worse than my armpits. I can smell *his* breath from here, and it's like he's been chewing mint leaves and French-kissing the North Wind. It's the freshest fucking breath I've ever experienced.

"Great," I stall, "so what happens, now? We have a shouting match where you keep insisting that we should join forces, because we're the same—"

"We're not alike at all, actually."

"We are *literally* the same person! You have a birthmark on your taint, right? You have a scar on your arm where you tried to burn off your freckles once, because some girl said they looked like dirt... and you were left-handed, but those studio school assholes made you do everything with your right hand, and that's why you can only really use your left hand when you're acting—"

He nods at all the things. Points a gun at me with his left hand. "Does this look like acting?" He fires.

I spin so fast I fall on my ass facing the mean librarian, who slumps against the wall with a neat hole in her forehead, just above her right eye.

"And," I say, "I got nothing."

"Good," he shouts thoughtfully over the ringing in my ears, "then you're ready." He strolls over to a wet bar set in an alcove and brings me a tall, frothy fruit smoothie. I detect pineapple, bananas, coconut, apple juice, spirulina, acetylcholine, 5-HTP and a stiff dose of ketamine.

While I suck it down, he infodumps, "We control everything, now. Everybody is living the dream. Invested heavily in interactive VR when everybody else thought it was just for video games, and when all the sex scandals cratered the studios, we swept up some of the most beloved intellectual properties in the industry for pennies on the dollar. Then we led the way to get Hollywood backing Republicans."

"Wipe wood ewe...?" I ask, staring into my smoothie.

He smiles. "Drink up. We realized it was almost impossible to make virtual reality so perfect that people would want to live in it permanently, but it was easy and cheap to make reality so unbearable that people would plead with us for any available exit.

"Everybody had the attention span of a gnat when they were all working to keep up, but now everybody's obsolete, they just want to curl up and live inside their fantasies. So we rolled out livable interactive environments of their favorite TV shows and movies on a subscription basis." A previously invisible flunkie holds up an iPad to present a slideshow of travel agent posters for Riverdale, Sunnydale, Hogwarts, Gotham City, Mayberry, Disney After Dark, Twin Peaks, The Shire, Westeros, Kardashiopolis and Guy Fieri's Flavortown.

"Hollywood doesn't make movies anymore and TV is all reruns in Spanish, but the industry is posting record returns on VR, and ninety-three percent of that revenue comes to us. Eighty million Americans list one of our domains as their primary residence. Four of our domains are on *USA Today's* Top 10 Most Livable Cities list this year. In the real world, they live under bridges, but in ours, they're knights and superheroes and celebrities who never get old and fat as they fight crime, molest Disney princesses and murder Laura Palmer."

"Let them eat Life Juice," I say, but it comes out sideways.

"When they can't pay up, they work for us as scripted characters, and pretty soon, they'll be able to sign over their bodies, sell their organs and limbs, for permanent residency. Junkies have been known to pawn their oxycodone prescriptions to stay in our programs, Honeycunt. Think about that. We've got 'em hooked harder than heroin. And don't get me started on the third-party porn mods, and the ancillaries for teledildonic packages.

"You know what the most popular domains are? *Walking Turds* and *Joan of Arkansas* are huge in the red states. People pay to live every waking moment in a wasteland blowing away poop-zombie Jane Fondas and locust abortion technicians and fucking each other over for virtual bullets and Bible credits."

"Those are my ideas!"

"Our ideas, dumbass. But *I* did something with them. *The Foxy Boxer* won nine Oscars, including Best Actor and Best

Actress for Jade Leto. *The Slotter House* is in its fifth season, and spun off a successful chain of feedlot-themed resort hotels. Somewhere right now, a homeless man living in a dishwasher box is nutting off with one of our VR rigs while the child version of us from *The Persons* slides a finger up his pooper. And I just made a dollar off it.

"Blue states are even better… Our *Social Justice Wasteland* community is big enough to demand its own congressional representation, but the idiots keep voting for Harambe and Pepe the Frog. It's just a buggy urban sandbox, but find enough red pills and get woke to the conspiracy, and you get superpowers and infinite ammunition. From there, they can port to the robot holocaust level and the Cave-Rave Orgy, and there's an infinite onion of nested dystopias, each more brutal, sexually ambivalent and semiotically didactic than the last. Millions of people love being rats in a maze, and our lab rats pay rent."

This is all fascinating, I try to tell him with my eyebrows, *but what do you need me for?*

He looks me in the eyes as long as he can stomach the view. "I need you to do me a favor. Then you can go back to your LA, and Mimi will throw open the gates. Anything you want, it'll happen."

Finally, we're back to shopworn movie clichés I can deal with. "What do I have to do?"

"Just perform an abortion."

"Yeah, so… um… no?"

"What, you've got a problem with abortion?"

"No, unless the mom doesn't want one… and this is all about protecting your weird, alternate-universe cult, isn't it?"

"I'm not from an alternate universe, Honeycunt… *You* are."

I have to count to 10. Naturally, he knows why I always hated my real name. "Fine," I say, projecting my foul, hungry breath into his face and savoring his scowl of disgust. "So… I have to do it instead of a licensed abortionist because…"

"You're as smart as me, allegedly; you figure it out."

"I have to do it so your sideshow pals think you're a badass, taking on the devil-spawn of the Improv comedy Messiah… but really, I need to do it because you're scared shitless of a baby."

"Good plotting, man. You could've made it as a screenwriter, if you learned how to read beyond *Everybody Poops*."

"Thanks. I was always my toughest critic, so that really means a lot." Without putting away the gun, he takes out a phone and punches up a video, holds it up.

I recognize Branko and Ivo, the Blood Eagle bunch. They're bolt upright on a couch. Eyes staring into the abyss. Blood squirts from a burst capillary in Branko's left tear duct, a lazy, arrhythmic trickle down his slack face and neck. Ivo's jaws work mechanically, stripping off the last shreds of his lips and joylessly chewing and swallowing them.

"Yeah, that's encouraging. But I've never even played a doctor on TV…"

"You don't need to get your hands dirty. You just have to make a fist of your mind and crush it. Like a bug."

"Sounds easy when *you* say it. But I'm not psychic, either. If you can do all that rad *Scanners* shit, why don't you?"

"You have the power, because I do. If I have to demonstrate it on you, you'll be in no shape to do what I need you to do. Are you going to do this thing, or not?"

The door opens, but the guards have to really shove it to get the mean librarian's corpse out of the way. They step over her and take me by my arms and lift me until only my toes are scraping the floor.

"You know why you failed as an actor? Because actors never imitate people, they imitate acting. All your life, what've you really wanted to be?"

Really? Physical abuse *and* a harsh personal inventory? "An actor? Duh… I mean, at least I'd never stoop to improv comedy."

"Because you can't do it."

"Shut up…"

"Because you watched movies and studied actors to learn how to portray emotion…"

"Shut up!"

"And *they* studied other actors who learned some bullshit acting technique at the knee of yet another actor."

"Shut the fuck up!"

"You never had any emotions of your own, except the wanting, did you? Everything real in your life that happened to you, you ignored or blocked or buried it, because it got in the way of the bullshit version of yourself you tried to become. Your whole life wasted getting in front of the camera, and did you ever have anything to share with the world besides, *Hey, Look at me!*? Did you ever stop to ponder how many removes you've gone astray from experiencing or expressing even the most basic, genuine human emotion?"

"I'm feeling one right now," I say.

"But you'll never learn from it, because you were always an actor. You want to succeed so bad, you can't even admit to yourself that you already had it all, and crashed and burned!"

"SHUT! UP!"

"You were Shinobi Honeycutt, the rottenest child star ever to drop out of junior high school. And you've been running from it ever since, but where did you get to? A new face, but you came right back to the same sewer, and you dove right back in."

TWENTY-EIGHT

From the *Deluxe Psylosophy Pioneer Lectures of Xavier Doderlik*, vol. 37 (Expanded Platinum Gift Box Edition)

DON'T ACT NATURAL, for fuck's sake. If people wanted to see people act natural, they could stand to look at each other.

Take a look at people when they don't know they're on camera, and you will come to believe a not particularly bright creator did indeed fashion us out of mud. Jacked off in one hand and shat in the other and, *Clap! Squish!* Humanity.

Acting isn't acting natural. They do things never for themselves or for others, but for the Moment. Actors spend their whole lives turned inside out, living like there is always a camera, like someone is watching and must be entertained by their most private, secret moments. They walk into every room like they own it, and leave every room like they just sold it for twice market value to a moron. They say exactly what you could never find the words to say in the right moment, and they can sell any emotion with any words, because they've rehearsed them until they're nothing but music and color and sex. They heroicaly hold their mud under pressure when useless shits like you would break down and make yourself repulsive to the camera.

You wouldn't last a second in a movie. Sniveling cowards and idiots only exist in movies to die and show the audience how sharp the world's teeth are.

Acting is how people would live if they knew God was watching their every move. Really watching.

Because you're creating the only thing in this universe that God can't create. The rarest element... what is it?

[Audience shouts: Truth? Beauty? Wisdom?]

DRAMA!

God is a monster and He's getting bored. All this space with nothing happening, all this meaningless shit whirling round the universe, and then there's us. And everything He does is just a kid pulling wings off flies until the flies start to sing.

And *you're fucking BORING HIM*!

You getting anything from this, any of you? [Throws clipboard into audience; someone crying] Sometimes, the kindest thing you can do for someone is to kill them, eat them and pass their energy back into the world to make something better.

[Nervous laughter]

Figuratively, of course.

But seriously... the greatest actor I've ever known used to have this trick for waking up his fellow actors, and even though he used to get in trouble for it, it was the most ingenious technique ever invented for forcing someone to be present...

To demonstrate, I'm going to need a volunteer...

In an interview for *TV Guide's* 1992 *Fall Preview Special* that was suppressed by his management when Season 2 of *The Persons* was axed, Shinobi tersely said of the goosing controversy, "They were all sleepwalking. I was just doing that to wake them up. People forget that everybody poops... they're not so special just because the shits they take end up on TV..."

 —*Spoiled Rotten*, Chapter 14—"Nasty, Brutish & Short"

TWENTY-NINE

[CUES: Jacques Lussier, "les dernier train du Katanga" from *Dark Of The Sun* Soundtrack; Todd Terje w/ Bryan Ferry, "Johnny & Mary"]

SO I'M RIDING IN THIS GOLFCART WITH SOME uniformed goons like they have in every old James Bond film. We're driving down a long white-tiled tunnel running under the LA River, the 5 and Griffith Park to connect the Forest Lawn franchises for easy, convenient supervillainy.

Just going to see my best gal and try to murder her dirty bomb of an unborn baby messiah with psychic powers I don't actually have.

But as the contents of the smoothie start to activate, it gets easier to believe I'm starting to have them, now. My mind is racing in elaborate slaloms and neon mazes, snapping off ideas like I've never experienced before, such startling new connections and revelations, that I'm moved to share them with the uniformed goons, but my mouth won't have any part of it.

"Blubber impala teeth are full wee salvia," I say meaningfully to the driver. I try again. "Hemp acne... lug nuts, Empanadas... Bug and pimp Kathy..." Every time, it comes out stupider, until I'm gargling my own tongue and the driver tells me to sweat the Yuk pup.

But it's so clear in my mind, so bright and shiny, if I could just rip the lid off my skull, I could fucking show him the

WORDS, so I just look at him and make the message extra bright in my head so he can see it right through my face.

LOVE AND EMPATHY ARE ALL WE HAVE

The driver hurls himself from the golfcart. We swerve and come to a squeaking halt. The driver runs screaming back up the tunnel to Glendale. The other goon raps me on the head with the gun and gets in the driver's seat.

Drives with the gun in my face, looking at me sideways real weird, like he can't believe he's pointing a gun at a guy who's a dead ringer for his personal savior. He gets used to it by the time we go up a ramp to emerge in a big open space like a former aquifer tank, because he hits me a couple times in the face for no cause at all. "Don't get any ideas," he says.

A couple ladies in white nurse's uniforms meet me and, with eyes averted and backs rigid, escort me into a labyrinth. The goon stays close behind with his gun in my back. Nobody else seems to notice, looking away from the Holiest of Holies when he comes shuffling in.

I'm led to a scrub room where they peel off my clothes, bathe me with moist towelettes and dress me in scarlet cotton scrubs.

Finally, they tell me the patient is ready, and await my instructions. "Yeah, um," I say, "let's go...?"

Maybe emboldened by my mellow mood, one of the nurses leans in close as she pulls thick rubber gloves onto each of my hands.

"May I tell the Master a joke?"

I look around. The goon looks at the ceiling. The other nurses glare with jealousy at the bold one, who starts to look scared the longer I take to find my mouth and pull an answer out.

"Sure, I lumber... lampreyjack... love jacking awful... I mean *Joe Kidd*."

Practically cooing, the nurse asks, "Why don't Hecklers celebrate their birthdays?"

Oh boy. "I... gadget up—giddyup... Swell meat, peach."

"Because their heads are so far up their asses, they think they haven't been born yet!"

CODY GOODFELLOW

I laugh easily enough, just looking into her eyes. She wants it so bad—no, she's scared to death. I wipe my eye, pretending her joke made me tear up. I say something that sounds nothing like, *That was pretty good, but wasn't it really more of a riddle?*

Her face falls. Before I can reach out to comfort her, the goons pounce on her, truss her up and trundle her off.

I—that other I—probably orders them to tell him jokes, and then punishes them when they don't make him laugh. Shitty, but it totally sounds like something I'd do, sooner or later, if people let me.

The silence hangs around our necks, so I blurt the first dumb one-liner that comes to mind. I try to say, *She's so dumb, she tried to put a dimmer switch on a TV so she could understand Sesame Street,* and everyone laughs like hyenas on nitrous, the most desperate sound I've ever heard in my life, all the way down to the big steel vault door of the nethermost bunker in the Forest Lawns Hollywood Hills Temple of Psylosophy. When the vault door closes behind me and I see them watching through the double-paned glass, I can look up and down their faces without finding their eyes, read their lips asking each other what the fuck *Sesame Street* and a *dimmer switch* are.

So I can't talk for shit, but my brain seems to be broadcasting just fine.

"Hi."

I turn around and a curtain retreats on a track and there she is, reclining on a white examination table with her legs akimbo under the trembling bulge of her enormous baby-belly.

"I'd feel better if I had some music," she says, "but my phone stopped working, and they took it away."

Biting my lip, I ask, *"Flat wood... Erm..."* Struggling, I force out, *"What... would you play... for this scene?"*

Her eyes widen. "I don't know... No music feels right in here, but something fun and sunny..."

"King Crimson is india ghoul..."

"Don't you know anything from your own lifetime?"

"I Matmos spiffy," I say. The ketamine is coming on stronger. I try to focus on the baby, on the *Pictures*.

Be Psychic, stupid.

I put my fingers to my temple the way you do in movies to show you're being psychic. I try to tell it, *Relax, I'm here to save you and your Mom—*

She lets out a piercing scream.

YOU MUST DELIVER ME, OR THIS WORLD, THESE LIVES, ARE LOST

The thought hits me like a sack of cement. I stagger backwards and sit down hard on the floor. *I don't know how to do that… You're the Messiah… Save yourself, why don't you? Isn't that what Messiahs are supposed to do?*

MY MIND HAS NOT MATURED MY BODY IS FRAIL MY MOTHER IS KIND OF A NUTJOB ONLY YOU CAN OVERCOME YOUR DARK DOPPELGANGER THE USURPER AND SET ME FREE—

Shit, I don't know… Maybe if I had some proof…

ASK ME ANYTHING

I walk over to the girl, standing so I block the window, then pull the curtain around the bed.

"Hey, what're you doing?" My evil twin demands over the intercom.

"*I can't do it with you looking!*" I call out. The gang outside the window stumbles like the bridge just soaked up a direct photon torpedo hit.

I put my hand on her belly. *How many times did I just tap you?*

A stirring under my fingers.

FOUR DO YOU BELIEVE ME NOW?

I trace an answer on her belly.

WHY DON'T YOU ANSWER?

I just answered you. I turn around and look at the window. Really look at it.

I was thinking *four*, but I didn't tap her belly at all. The answer I wrote was NONE.

Whipping aside the curtain, I go to look at the people

outside the window. Hungry, empty improv actor faces. Only one of them has trouble keeping up that maddening, crooked Dreamworks animation grin. It's the goon who rode with me on the golfcart, the one I couldn't bamboozle.

When I look at him, really, look, I see the intern who subtly guided me through the talkshow cattle call and ditched me right next to her.

And then I see who he really is.

I'm gonna need some volunteers from the audience. I point right at him. *You. Come in here and give me a hand.*

He looks startled, steps back into the clutches of two guys who put a menacing ice bucket on his head.

My evil twin steps into view. "I *knew* it. I knew the superbaby act was a sham. Thanks for airing him out for us."

So, what about us?

"Suck all the air out of the room," my evil twin says. The prospect of watching himself die like a shelter dog pitches a tent in his pants. Like I needed any more reasons to loathe myself—

The vents hiss and it starts getting cold.

"NO! Don't do it!" I go to the door and put my hand on the knob and it opens. My evil twin rages at his own cupidity in having biometric scanners put on all the important doors.

My evil twin backs away as his guards seize the jerk who ruined my whole day.

"*Hey, you assholes! Don't let him hurt that guy! He's the real Xavier Doderlik! He's your fucking messiah!*"

The others flatten against the wall, shaking their heads to clear my sloppy telepathic stain from their brains. My evil twin clenches his buttocks and glares at me with narrowed eyes. "Did you just goose me?"

"Not... physically, no..."

He comes over and kicks me in the shin, then in the crotch. As I fall, he leans in close. "I've always dreamed of killing myself," he says.

"Don't let me stop you," I tell him. "But first..."

"Yes?" He takes out a long lobotomy poker as his guards

pin me to the floor.

"You really need a breath mint."

He blanches, covers his mouth with his hand. "Do I, really? Is it that bad?"

"Yeah. Like dogshit in a hot car in summer bad."

"Jesus fucking Christ, why doesn't anyone ever *say anything*?" He takes the breath mint out of my hand, and puts it in his mouth. "OK, where were we? Oh yeah… lobotomy…"

He raises the spike above my eye, but then he stops, jaw working, looking at me as if I was trying to talk him into this whole thing, but he just stops—

He smacks his lips, burps and makes a disgusted face. "What the hell am I doing? This is awful. I'm in a position to share wisdom and spiritual technology, and I've only used it to pursue my own empty self-aggrandizement. This is…" He throws the spike away. "Let him up. Let that man go, he's the savior of us all."

The guards hesitantly let me get up and take the bucket off Doderlik's head.

My evil twin hugs his erstwhile mentor, gushing telepathically all over the room. *I'm so glad you're here, Master. I've just awakened to so many things, and with you here, we can really do everything good that every organized religion ever failed at. We can create a paradise on earth.*

"Sure," Doderlik says, then turns to the guard. "Execute him." Before my twin can catch his breath, he's shot six times and drops in a heap at Doderlik's feet.

Doderlik turns to me. "We could probably make life real interesting for each other, but one of you was one too many for this planet, and I don't even want to risk having your corpse here. So please, wherever you came from… go back. And take her with you."

"Asshole," the girl says. "What about *us*?" She thrusts out her baby bump. "What about *this*?"

He looks at her as if he honestly can't, for the life of him, remember where he's seen her before. "I already said, you can go. Thanks for your help."

"But you do share some responsibility, you know…"

"Fine." To the guards, "Cut her a check and drop her off at the clinic on Ventura and Coldwater. Put it up for adoption, or whatever."

"So that's it? None of it meant *anything* to you? All those things you said about the baby, about us… All of those things the baby…" Trying not to cry, "Things he told me… None of it?"

"Lady, I've worked my whole life to develop my mental powers, and even so, it's taken me until now to be comfortable in my own skin, and in charge of a major religion that, last time I checked, was the only one still legal in this version of California. Pretty sweet. And then there's you.

"What's wrong with this picture? The devastatingly handsome, brilliant messiah of humankind and his chubby, knock-kneed nobody peasant wife from Wherever, Washington…"

"Wenatchee!"

"Go back there, because there's no place for you in this or any other LA. Because you're the only unforgivable sin incarnate. You're *ordinary*. You're everything we left behind when we came here to realize our dreams. You're the cute girl who seems like a catch, and skips her pills once before prom, and ruins your whole life. You and your kind have killed more dreams than Hitler and Stalin and the Church, combined! So go and get scraped and go home, or go and raise your bastard, with my regards. I bequeath unto him my nearsightedness, my fallen arches, my webbed toes and pattern baldness, but unless I ever find myself in need of spare parts, I don't see how I'll have any need for a son, so…"

WAAAAAAAAAAAAAAAH!

We all feel it. It goes through everything like the thunder from a direct lightning strike, as close as your zipper.

We all feel it, but it isn't for us.

Doderlik's head implodes, abruptly shrinking to the size and color of a stewed beet.

"OK," I say, resting one hand on the girl's belly. "Anyone

else want to give us shit?"

I wheel her out of the bunker into a huge room full of NASA-type junk. She's sulking. I don't want to get into it with this chick, but I want to talk to the one I see on the other end of the room even less.

"What's your problem? We won!"

"It sure doesn't feel like it. That guy's a total dick… and you didn't stick up for me at all, and worst of all, I feel like a *thing*. Like I was just a womb for that asshole to put a baby in, and only an object for you to run around trying to save, and now I'm going to be a mother alone in a place where nobody gives a shit about anyone else…"

"Well, giving birth is pretty heroic."

"Bullshit, it just happens. It comes out whether or not you push, you know. It's not like getting through college, or buying a house or quitting drinking."

"*I* couldn't do it."

"You could if you were a woman. We have a higher pain tolerance, another layer of endodermis, we're built to take it… fuck, I need *drugs*."

"OK, you win." I push her chair through the media room, towards Mimi, whose dogs are sitting in the chairs, fucking with the controls.

"Nice job," she says.

"So what about me? What do I get?"

"I told you not to book this gig, that there was no money in it."

"THERE'S NEVER ANY MONEY."

"Right. Well, I can still give you what you wanted." She points to a little dais with a bunch of laser-pointer things suspended over it. The Lurcks herd me up onto it, then the girl.

I lean in close as if I'm going to kiss her, and for just a moment, she seems ready to surrender to destiny. A blinding flash consumes us, and then everything goes dark.

"That's all we need," Mimi says. "Get the fuck out. We won't be in touch."

I push the girl up a ramp and out onto the plaza where the marble statue of Doderlik lies facedown in the delphinium bed, and the gigantic hologram foot is gone.

And in its place...

She stands almost two miles high, the moon eclipsed by the looming, apocalyptic harvest moon of her belly.

She draws in a breath and says, "Oh, it's beautiful." Then, "Hey, I don't even know your name..."

I try to answer her, but I can't, for looking into the west, at the other hologram.

It stands maybe a mile taller than the Glendale one, and it's not nearly so lovely to look at, but I can't look away, and no matter what I look at, I'll never stop seeing it.

It's *me*.

Standing on the shoulder of the Hollywood Hills cemetery and holding out my hands, leaning in for a kiss that will not come until we are all dead and gone and the stars go out. An always-coming kiss that will be remembered as the sacrament of a new religion... but a good one, with characters you can root for, a happy ending and a killer soundtrack.

She smiles and takes my hand and I turn to her and close my eyes and start to bend over, when she moans, "Oh God, I think it's starting..."

I step back, rubbing my temples. I can barely hear her for the lower, deeper, louder roar in my head. A roar like an ocean, like a wave rolling back and rearing up to drown the stars.

"I'm just gonna... go," I say, "get... help..."

I run across the plaza to the mausoleum, but I run into a blind wall instead of the stairs, and when I turn around again and go out, the statue in the plaza is a replica of Michelangelo's David, and the unobstructed moon and a dozen or so stars are out and an Alaska Airlines 767 passes close by, on final approach to Bob Hope Airport.

A few wilted wreaths with half-empty foil balloons that say GET WELL SOON are settled around a fairly recent grave.

I piss on the flowers without reading the name and then head south, into the hills where the last manicured meadow turns to trackless coastal desert scrub and the coyotes howl over the latest victim of Hollywood.

I may not have any useful knowledge or wisdom to share with the world, but I know what we do is a sacred trust more vital to humanity than any doctor, lawyer or priest.

Whatever shitty time-wasting entertainment vehicle we might ride into your hearts, be it a lousy slasher, a desperate porno or a maddening infomercial created only to steal your time and money, even when the rest of the program says relax, have another beer, we live to remind you life is short, so look into our eyes as we burn for you.

We step on the altar, and break our bodies and minds to set ourselves on fire in limelight to remind you that no matter what you buy, sell or take to ease the pain; no matter who you worship or vote for; no matter how you fuck your head into forgetting the truth, YOU WILL NOT LIVE FOREVER.

If we each become the bold but not-an-asshole hero in the movie of our life, we might find true love, capture fame and fortune, win the lottery and save the universe; but we might die tonight, too. Or we can stay home and play the one-dimensional walk-on hacked out by a bored character actor in someone else's movie.

THIRTY
[Cue: Hot Butter, "At The Movies"]

I STAGGER INTO HOLLYWOOD AT DAWN.

My pants torn and bristling with stickers, burrs and coyote shit from my trek through Griffith Park. I stopped at the Hollywood sign and took a piss under the big D, where some beatnik genius once played Hawaiian castaway in the hills while he wrote "Nature Boy" for Nat King Cole and picked out hit singles for Capitol. More red than yellow. Maybe that's a good sign. Maybe not.

I'm sitting at the counter at 101 Coffee Shop when some baby-faced guy in a disheveled Armani suit comes over and offers to pay for my Belgian waffle and gravy.

Nice, as I have no cash and was fixing to dash on it. But what's the deal? I'm not into rough trade, but for a reasonable fee, I can put him onto a handy little guy with removable teeth and an extensive wig collection.

"You're really for real," says the guy, pausing to chuckle and punch me in the shoulder, "aren't you? No, what I'm after is, I was, I mean—we were—watching you when you came in. And seriously, I know how this sounds, you know… but I'm repping this dynamite script for an indie I think could open Sundance, with the right lead. And something about you tells me you'd be right for this."

He takes it out and shows it to me. "We own the rights to the book, but we didn't take much from it, since there's so little, really, to know. We call it a 'radical speculative biopic.' Like, jumping off from when he vanished, like D.B. Cooper, and he has all these misadventures... You know, like what if he's still out there, fucking shit up?"

I flip through the script a couple times, then run my fingers over the title: MAKE-BELIEVE WASTELAND (by some asshole you've never heard of) BASED ON SPOILED ROTTEN: THE SHORT LIFE AND BIZARRE ENIGMA OF A LITTLE HOLLYWOOD MONSTER by some other douchebag who shall remain forever nameless.

"I know it's weird, just out of the blue like this, but we think the timing is right, and we just, from the moment you walked in, like I said..."

I take a long, deep breath. "I'd love to work with you..."

"That's awesome!" He squeezes my arm and turns to give a thumbs-up to a couple more hungover young producers in a corner booth.

"It's the part I was born to play, seriously. But I can tell you already, I'm gonna have some notes for you on the script."

A bit dubiously, "Are you, now?"

"Yeah." I take a big sip of coffee and make him wait, feel his attention flowing into me like hot, caffeinated blood. "For starters, your title sucks..."

[CUE: Tokimonsta, "Put It Down"]
SMASH CUT TO WHITE

END CREDITS

AN ERASERHEAD PRESS PRESENTATION
OF A CODY GOODFELLOW BOOK

WRITTEN by
CODY GOODFELLOW

EDITED by
ROSE O'KEEFE

PRODUCTION DESIGN
MATTHEW REVERT

NEGATIVE CUTTER
ALICIA GRAVES

I'D LIKE TO THANK...
My agent, Gail Marx and everybody at Daily Talent; my
voiceover coach, Bill Holmes; Cameron Pierce; John Skipp,
Andrew Kasch, Frank Woodward and Jack Bennett; the cast
& crew of Anthrax, "Blood Eagle Wings" and Beck, "Wow";
Aquarius; *American Horror Story: Roanoke*; *Best Friends
Whenever*; *Kirby Buckets*; *Shameless*; *Shooter*; *You're The Worst*;
Gorgeous Ladies Of Wrestling; *Kevin Hart's Guide To Black
History* and *The Conan O'Brian Show*.

CODY GOODFELLOW has written six solo novels and three with NY Times bestselling author John Skipp. Two collections of his short fiction, *Silent Weapons For Quiet Wars* and *All-Monster Action*, received the Wonderland Book Award. He wrote, co-produced and scored the short Lovecraftian hygiene film *Stay At Home Dad*. As a bishop of the Esoteric Order of Dagon, he presides over several Cthulhu Prayer Breakfasts each year. He once played an Amish farmer in a Days Inn commercial, and has appeared in the background on numerous TV programs, including *Aquarius, Shooter, American Horror Story: Roanoke, G.L.O.W., You're The Worst, Kirby Buckets* and Kevin Hart's *Guide To Black History*. He is also a cofounder of Perilous Press, an occasional micropublisher of modern cosmic horror. He currently lives in Portland, Oregon.